HARLEQUIN®
Presents

In Harlequin Presents books seduction and passion are always guaranteed, and this month is no exception! You'll love what we have to offer you this April....

Favorite author Helen Bianchin brings us *The Marriage Possession*, where a devilishly handsome millionaire demands his pregnant mistress marry him. In part two of Sharon Kendrick's enticingly exotic THE DESERT PRINCES trilogy, *The Sheikh's Unwilling Wife*, the son of a powerful desert ruler is determined to make his estranged wife resume her position by his side.

If you love passionate Mediterranean men, then these books will definitely be ones to look out for! In Lynne Graham's *The Italian's Inexperienced Mistress*, an Italian tycoon finds that one night with an innocent English girl just isn't enough! Then in Kate Walker's *Sicilian Husband, Blackmailed Bride*, a sinfully gorgeous Sicilian vows to reclaim his wife in his bed. In *At the Greek Boss's Bidding*, Jane Porter brings you an arrogant Greek billionaire whose temporary blindness leads to an intense relationship with his nurse.

And for all of you who want to be whisked away by a rich man... *The Secret Baby Bargain* by Melanie Milburne tells the story of a ruthless multimillionaire returning to take his ex-fiancée as his wife. In *The Millionaire's Runaway Bride* by Catherine George, the electric attraction between a vulnerable PA and her wealthy ex proves too tempting to resist.

Finally, we have a brand-new author for you! In Abby Green's *Chosen as the Frenchman's Bride* a tall, bronzed Frenchman takes an innocent virgin as his wife. Be sure to look out for more from Abby very soon!

*Legally wed,
but he's never said,
"I love you."
They're...*

**The series where marriages are made
in haste...and love comes later.**

**Look out for more WEDLOCKED!
wedding stories available only from
Harlequin Presents®**

Helen Bianchin

THE MARRIAGE POSSESSION

HARLEQUIN®

TORONTO • NEW YORK • LONDON
AMSTERDAM • PARIS • SYDNEY • HAMBURG
STOCKHOLM • ATHENS • TOKYO • MILAN • MADRID
PRAGUE • WARSAW • BUDAPEST • AUCKLAND

ISBN-13: 978-0-373-12619-4
ISBN-10:   0-373-12619-0

THE MARRIAGE POSSESSION

First North American Publication 2007.

All about the author...
Helen Bianchin

HELEN grew up in New Zealand, an only child possessed by a vivid imagination and a love for reading. After four years of legal secretarial work, Helen embarked on a working holiday in Australia, where she met her Italian-born husband, a tobacco sharefarmer in far north Queensland. His command of English was pitiful, and her command of Italian was nil. Fun? Oh yes! So too was being flung into cooking for workers immediately after marriage, stringing tobacco and living in primitive conditions.

It was a few years later when Helen, her husband and their daughter returned to New Zealand, settled in Auckland and added two sons to their family. Encouraged by friends to recount anecdotes of her years as a tobacco sharefarmer's wife living in an Italian community, Helen began setting words on paper and her first novel was published in 1975.

Creating interesting characters and telling their stories remains as passionate a challenge for Helen as it did in the beginning of her writing career.

Spending time with family, reading and watching movies are high on Helen's list of pleasures. An animal lover, Helen says her Maltese terrier and two Birman cats regard her study as much theirs as hers.

CHAPTER ONE

THE legal soirée was invitation-only, hosted in a luxurious hotel and presented for the city's legal eagles and their partners.

Judges, barristers and eminent lawyers of note. Where friendships flourished and opponents left the rigours of the court-room behind.

'More champagne?'

The familiar male drawl had the power to quicken Lisane's heartbeat…and more, so much more.

Lisane tilted her head a little, met Zac's dark, gleaming eyes, and almost drowned in their depths. 'Do I appear to need it?'

A loaded query, if ever there was one!

Mingling with her peers would be a breeze in comparison with the formal dinner, where seating arrangements would place her at Zac's side in the company of his parents, and Allegra Fabrisi, their preferred choice of a partner for their son.

Tonight she would field empty compliments, the brilliant female smiles that didn't reach the eyes…each of which were a mere salutation in deference to attract the attention of the man at her side.

Zacharias Winstone, wealthy in his own right, a prominent barrister and son of an eminent judge, he was the embodiment of everything that was charismatic male.

In his late thirties, tall, with dark hair and dark eyes, broad-shouldered, wide-boned, sculptured features, a sensual mouth and piercing dark eyes, didn't come close to describing the inherent sensuality he projected with effortless ease.

Zac, the babe magnet.

One had only to *look* at him to *know* he could drive a woman wild. It was there in his eyes, the faint, teasing smile … the promise, simmering beneath the sophisticated façade.

Women undressed him with one lingering, seductive look, and blatantly moved in for the kill. For some it was a challenge, others had more serious plans in mind… So far none had been successful.

For the moment he was *hers*. Friend, lover…

Commitment wasn't a word Zac mentioned and *marriage* didn't enter the equation.

Relationship? Lisane pondered the word, sought its true meaning, and failed to pin it down.

Together…for now, seemed appropriate.

A pensive smile tilted the edge of her mouth.

It was enough…wasn't it?

They shared much, yet in many ways were poles apart.

His wealth earned him a position on an accredited list of Australia's wealthiest names, while she came from an ordinary family of humble means and her education had been gained via scholarships and part-time work to help pay expenses.

Within the legal profession, Zac was recognised as one of the best in his field of criminal law…while Lisane occupied a position in the Crown Prosecutor's office.

He had chambers in Brisbane, resided in a city apartment and owned a magnificent waterfront mansion on Sovereign Islands, an élite suburb on Queensland's Gold Coast, seventy kilometres distant.

Vastly different from the small, weathered cottage in fashionable suburban Milton that Lisane had bought, mortgaged and was in the process of renovating.

A Sydney-based girl of French-born parents, she'd relocated to Brisbane a year ago…a move due in part to the need for change. And the desire to remove herself from what had become an awkward situation.

Two couples…two blonde, blue-eyed sisters dating two brothers. Except whereas Solene and Jean-Claude had fallen in love and planned to marry, Lisane didn't share the same feelings for Alain. Friendship, yes, and affection. But not love.

Something it had taken a while to divine, given the almost life-long connection. Solene's engagement to Jean-Claude had prompted Alain's marriage proposal, and Lisane accepted his ring, temporarily caught up in Alain's persuasion and her sister's euphoria…only to have doubt soon cloud her perspective.

It hadn't been easy to break off the engagement, nor to leave the city of her birth. Except it wouldn't have been fair to Alain to stay.

He deserved more. So did she.

The law had fascinated Lisane from an early age, fostered and shaped by gritty television police and court-room dramas…none of which bore much resemblance to reality, she reflected with a tinge of wry amusement.

At twenty-seven, she hadn't found it difficult to settle into a new job in a different city. In many ways she'd relished the changes, new faces, forming tentative friendships…and running into Zac.

Literally. Three days after assuming her position in the Crown Prosecutor's office.

The momentous occasion had occurred in the city courthouse when she exited from the lift on the wrong floor.

It had taken only seconds to realise her mistake, and she'd swiftly turned…only to collide with a hard male frame.

An immediate apology had left her lips, and in the same instant she became aware of the man's physical impact… his impressive height, breadth of shoulder, his sculptured facial features. Not to mention the fine quality of his clothing, the faint aroma of his cologne. The slight smile curving his sensuously moulded mouth. And foremost, his indisputable aura of power.

Definitely off the Richter scale in terms of the *wow* factor, she had acknowledged a few minutes later as she rode the lift to the correct floor.

Who was he?

Discovery hadn't taken long. The family *Winstone* was well-known in legal and social circles. Zac Winstone was a legend in both.

The fact he sought her out had seemed little short of amazing. So, too, had his invitation to join him for coffee. A week or two later it had been followed by dinner, then a show…

'Pleasant thoughts, I hope?'

Lisane spared him a stunning smile. 'Why shouldn't they be?'

He was something else. Tuned in to her in a way that made her wonder if he'd become adept at reading her mind. Although pure people skills, the ability to weigh up character traits and successfully divine them, contributed much to his success in the court-room. Very little, if anything, seemed to escape him.

Zac curled his fingers through her own, and leant in close. 'Just remember I get to take you home.'

A teasing light entered her eyes. 'That's supposed to see me through the next few hours?'

'It won't?'

His place or hers. It hardly mattered which, as long as they shared what remained of the night together.

'The jury's still out.'

His soft laughter almost undid her. 'Let's commence the tour of duty, shall we?'

Zac's parents, Max and Felicity Winstone, had just entered the large lounge area, followed, Lisane saw, by Leo Fabrisi, his wife, Charmaine, and their daughter, Allegra.

Two brilliant judges married to two equally qualified solicitors, who had each borne a child destined to follow in their footsteps into law.

There was little doubt the coupling of Zac Winstone with Allegra Fabrisi would make a perfect match. Or that both sets of parents were intent on actively encouraging it. Allegra made no secret that snaring Zac was her prime focus.

Tonight the glamorous barrister had chosen a designer gown in sinful black which hugged her tautly honed curves like a second skin. Long, gleaming hair the colour of rich sable cascaded in loose waves halfway down her back, and even from this distance her make-up resembled perfection.

Wonderful.

Lisane couldn't compete. Her budget didn't allow for the purchase of designer originals, or the Manolo Blahnik or Jimmy Choo stilettos that inevitably graced Allegra's slender feet. And her jewellery was limited to a diamond pendant and matching ear-studs she'd inherited from her mother.

Fortunately, her talents included the skillful use of a sewing machine, and she doubted even the most observant society maven would spot that the exquisite gown in floral silk she wore had been fashioned by her own hand.

Muted music provided a pleasant background to the social chatter abounding among numerous patrons in the large lobby, and Zac's progress was frequently stalled as they paused to speak with a friend or associate.

Lisane briefly entertained the uncharitable thought that they might escape detection for a while longer, and thus delay a confrontation with the Winstone and Fabrisi parents.

Fat chance.

She watched with detached fascination as Zac's elegantly attired mother caught sight of her son, and began leading the group of five towards him.

'Darling.' Allegra stepped in close and pressed glossy lips to Zac's cheek. 'We're a little late.' Her mouth performed a pretty teasing pout. 'Traffic.' Dark, eloquently warm eyes assumed a cool tinge as she acknowledged the young woman at his side. 'Lisane.'

She bore Allegra's studied appraisal with a practised

smile before greeting each set of parents with a politeness gained from instilled good manners.

Wealth and social position lent that certain indefinable air some people exuded with an inborn ease acquired almost from birth. Maximilian Winstone, or Max, as he preferred to be known, could trace his ancestors back several centuries to an era of obscene wealth, enormous holdings and a social position almost second to none.

'Go fetch some champers, darling.' Allegra issued Zac the directive with a seductive look that was definite overkill. 'I need something to kick-start the evening.'

There were waiters and waitresses in abundance. Zac merely lifted a hand to catch attention, and within seconds a waiter bearing a tray of filled champagne flutes moved to their group.

Allegra wrinkled her perfectly shaped nose. 'Not, I think, the house variety.' She placed a beautifully lac-quered nail on Zac's arm. 'Shall we adjourn to the bar?'

'We're about to be seated.' His voice was even, yet there was a warning hint beneath the surface.

One Allegra chose to ignore.

'There'll be at least thirty minutes of boring speeches before they serve the first course. We've plenty of time.'

Lisane felt her body tense. For what? An intimate tête-à-tête? To cause a temporary division between her and Zac?

She should be used to Allegra's ploys, for they occurred at frequent intervals and without doubt were deliberately orchestrated to diminish Lisane's existence in Zac's life.

It was a relief to see the ballroom doors swing open, and they joined the mingling guests entering the large room.

Polite, superficially pleasant conversation tempered the evening, and the addition of a further three guests at their table provided some light relief from Allegra's not so subtle attempts to command Zac's attention.

The food was superb, although Allegra barely sampled a morsel from each course while sipping Cristal champagne.

Discretion and client privilege ensured that only generalities within the legal system were discussed, and Lisane did her best to appear interested in Charmaine and Allegra's recount of a recent shopping expedition in Sydney, where it seemed Allegra had been intent on adding to her collection of expensive shoes and bags.

'Prada, darling,' Allegra extolled. 'And the most gorgeous Louis Vuitton.' She subjected Lisane to a sweeping appraisal. 'Your gown. Is it a Collette Dinnigan?'

I wish! 'D'Aubigne.' It was her late mother's maiden name, and one she felt entitled to use.

An eyebrow slanted in overt puzzlement. 'I'm not familiar with the label.'

'It's French,' Lisane enlightened solemnly.

'Of course. One can tell from the superb craftsmanship.'

Lisane restrained the desire to smile. Allegra was completely unaware she'd inadvertently gifted a compliment.

It was almost a relief when the evening drew to a close. Allegra's attempts to monopolise Zac's attention had moved Lisane from mild amusement to irritation. Had the beautiful barrister no scruples?

Don't answer that!

The 'goodnight' process took a while, and Lisane felt her tension ease as she slid into the passenger seat of Zac's sleek Jaguar shortly before midnight.

Thank heavens for the weekend. It would allow time to put the finishing touches to the kitchen trim, then mid-week, when the laquer paint had hardened, she could hang the lace curtains.

The cottage was gradually coming together. She adored the homely country-style furniture and refurbishing she'd chosen. It suited the one-hundred-year-old wooden structure, and she'd painstakingly polished the wooden floors, added rugs and wall-hangings in cross-stitch and tapestry.

She could walk indoors and feel at peace with her surroundings. Her plans for the garden were underway, a vegetable patch already yielding some fine produce; and while she still had some work to complete in the flower borders, there was time to bring it to its full potential.

Tomorrow, after a lingering breakfast at one of the city's pavement cafés, Zac would deliver her home.

Tonight…what remained of the night was theirs.

Just the thought of how it would end caused her heartbeat to accelerate and heat to course through her veins.

Gentle fingers brushed her cheek, almost as if he sensed what she was thinking, and she covered his hand with her own for a few timeless seconds before releasing it to offer him a lingering smile.

The Jaguar swept down into the underground car park beneath the tall city apartment building and came to a smooth halt in Zac's designated space.

He took hold of her hand as they entered the lift and buried his lips in her palm. His eyes were almost black, and she was willing to swear her bones began to melt at the degree of emotion reflected in those dark depths.

She needed to have his mouth on hers…his hands on her body, moulding each sensitised breast, exploring pleasure pulses, bringing her sensual heart alive and aching…for him, only him.

The lift slid to a halt, and minutes later they entered Zac's luxurious apartment. Floor-to-ceiling glass provided a panoramic view of the city, myriad lights and bright neon winking against an indigo sky.

It was a sight which never failed to enchant her, and she crossed to the tempered glass and gazed beyond the cityscape to the darkened outline of distant hills.

There was piped background music cued in low, courtesy of Zac's sound system, and she turned as magnificent curtains swished closed from the touch of an electronic button.

Dimmed lighting provided soft illumination, turning the large lounge area into their own private world.

'Come here.' Zac's voice was deep, husky, and Lisane took hold of his outstretched hand.

He drew her in and held her close to his hard body, then lowered his head to nuzzle the sensitive skin beneath her earlobe.

'I've waited all night to be able to do this.'

Slow-dancing.

Lisane closed her eyes and let emotion take over her body. It felt so good to be like this with him. To breathe in his male scent beneath the fine tailoring; to have the freedom to slide her hands beneath his jacket and savour the heady warmth. *Feel* the hard musculature and sense the quickened beat of his heart.

This was where she wanted to be. With him. The physical whereabouts hardly mattered, nor did the soft, lilting music drifting from expensive speakers.

There was only the man, the heady, dreamy sensation, and the need to feel his hands, his lips on her body, arousing, with the promise of how the night would end…and the journey.

He was a generous lover, intent on gifting the ultimate in pleasure, and she swayed slightly, almost missing her step…and felt the slide of his hand to the base of her spine as he held her firm against him.

His arousal was a potent force, and she lifted her arms to encircle his neck, then sank in against him as he lowered his head down to hers.

Magic.

She felt his fingers loosen the slide-comb holding the length of her hair, sensed the silky fall of it around her shoulders, and the slow threading of his fingers through its length.

He adored the feel of it, the faint fresh smell of her favoured floral-scented shampoo. The way she tossed her head in the throes of passion, and the tumbled mass of waves that fell like a curtain across each cheek…or cascaded down her naked back as she arched up against him and flung back her head.

He could bury his face in its silky length and savour the sweetness…*her*.

Beautiful, so very beautiful inside and out. Intelligent, clever, yet without artifice or contrived coquetry.

He wanted her…in his life. In his bed. He hadn't given much thought for how long. There didn't seem to be the need. The status quo suited him…suited them both. He couldn't see any reason for anything to change.

Zac took the kiss deeper, and Lisane experienced the familiar deep pull of desire.

Had they stopped moving? She wasn't sure, didn't care.

All that mattered was his mouth on hers, possessing with such tactile skill she became lost. *His*, solely his in a way that rendered her wanton…and *wanting*.

His clothes, hers, were an inconvenient barrier they

each sought to remove. Urgent hands, accompanied by barely audible sounds as the need to feel skin-on-skin contact became unbearable, closely followed by the shimmering satisfaction as the last shred of silk slithered down onto the carpeted floor.

In one fluid movement she leapt up against him and curled her legs around his waist, and sensed rather than heard the soft, laughing groan deep in his throat.

Seconds later he eased his mouth free from her own and feathered light fingers down the length of her spine, teased the curves of her buttocks, then unerringly found the warm, moist heat of her.

Wickedly clever fingers sent her high, the spiralling sensation causing her to gasp with the intensity of it, and she clung on to him, unaware of the soft, guttural sounds emerging from her throat as he brought her to climax.

He reclaimed her mouth, sweeping the soft inner tissue with his tongue, before tangling with her own in an erotic exploration that mirrored the intimacy of sexual possession.

She wanted more...so much more, and she lowered her body a little so the intimate heart of her rested against his powerful arousal. Then she moved, slowly, in an evocative teasing slide that had his heartbeat thudding in his chest and rendered him almost without breath.

'Minx.'

A soft knowing laugh emerged from her throat. It had been Zac who'd taught her to totally relax and enjoy sex. To receive and gift pleasure without inhibition.

'Bite me.'

'Now, there's a thought.'

'Promises, huh?'

Lisane moved up against him, then gave a surprised

gasp as he adjusted her position, eased his length into the moist heart of her...and surged in to the hilt.

She was aware of stretched tissue, intimate muscles enclosing him...and their readiness to convulse at his slightest move.

'What are you waiting for?' Her query was a breathless murmur, and she felt the press of his mouth against the vulnerable curve of her neck.

'You. To catch up.'

'Wretch.' If he wanted a challenge, she'd give him one!

The move was hers, and she relished being in control... until he took over. Then nothing mattered except their escalating pleasure and a libidinous climax that shattered them both.

Afterwards he carried her into the shower, where they gently bathed each other beneath the pulsing water, then, once dry, they walked naked into the bedroom and slid beneath the cool percale sheets to indulge in a slow, sensuous after-play...drifting fingers sliding over smooth skin, the gentle brush of lips, and soft, indistinct murmurs of appreciation.

On the edge of sleep Lisane sighed a silent word of thanks. For the man who cradled her close, and the place she'd reached in her life.

It was good. Very good.

No other man had made her feel so aware of her emotional heart...or so *alive* and incredibly sensual.

There was a certain danger in analysing her feelings in depth, for she was wary of repeating her mistake with Alain.

Although what she shared with Zac was different...so very different.

Love?

She didn't want to go there. Dared not. For it would mean contemplating an admission of sorts...one she wasn't ready to make.

It was enough their togetherness lasted a while.

CHAPTER TWO

LISANE came awake to the feather-like drift of fingers teasing a path over one hip, and the breath caught in her throat as they slid a little and sought the warm, moist, intimate heart at the apex of her thighs.

Soft lips nuzzled the sensitive curve at the edge of her neck, and she felt her pulse thud to a quickened beat as those skilful fingers found the highly sensitised nub, stroking it gently until she arched against his hand, wanting, needing more.

'Good morning.'

Zac's musing drawl sounded close to her ear, and her mouth curved into a generous smile as she opened her eyes to look at him.

Tousled dark hair, beard-shadow darkening his sculptured facial features…those eyes, so warm and liquid brown, and a mouth to die for.

'It's Saturday.'

Silent laughter lightened his gaze and his lips curved a little. 'And this is important…because?'

'I get to do this.'

He'd taught her so much. Where to touch and how. She knew what caused his breath to hitch. The way his body

tensed when she enclosed his arousal and began to tantalise, driving him to the edge, the faint hiss as she brought
him close to climax in what became a test of his endurance.
The times he reached it and assumed control...the occasions when he allowed her to take charge.

Their loving was at times hungry, primitive, when
passion ruled and surpassed all else. Mostly, it was slow
and incredibly erotic, a true feast of the senses.

Lisane moved in close and brushed her lips to his
cheek. 'Do you have anything important planned for the
next hour?'

Zac moved a little so her mouth met his. 'Nothing
without you.'

Morning sex, Lisane mused as they rose from the bed,
was a great way to begin the day.

Together they shared a leisurely shower, then, towelled
dry, she followed him into the bedroom and collected fresh
underwear from her overnight bag and pulled on jeans and
a pink singlet, added a cropped top in black and slid her
feet into kitten heels.

With quick, smooth fingers she caught her hair into a
loose knot, applied minimum make-up, added a touch of
lip-gloss, then packed her overnight bag.

Zac took it from her hand, and trailed light fingers
down her cheek. 'Hungry?'

'Uh-huh.' Her eyes sparkled with mischievous humour.
'For food.'

He pressed a thumb-pad to her lower lip. 'Of course.'

She was something else. Intelligent, savvy and possessed of an innate honesty. What was more, there wasn't
an ounce of coquetry...which made for a refreshing
change from most young women of his acquaintance.

Together they decided on a Park Road café not far from Lisane's cottage, selected a pavement table and ordered a full breakfast, preluded by strong, hot coffee.

The sun shone brightly, promising a warm late-spring day, and there was a freshness in the air that would dissipate as the temperatures rose, along with the humidity.

It seemed almost a shame to consider spending most of the weekend indoors. For a moment Lisane thought wistfully of Zac's waterfront home at Sovereign Islands, his cruiser moored at the jetty, and the occasional weekend they'd spent together there when the constraints of work had allowed them free time.

'More coffee?'

Lisane was seriously tempted to delay their departure, and it helped a little to know she could. Except she knew time was an important factor, given Zac was engaged in a particularly difficult case, one that required long, tedious hours as he meticulously built undisputed evidence and framed his questioning technique in preparation for a trial due soon to go to court.

'I'm fine.' She slid her sunglasses into place from atop her head, and rose to her feet. 'It's time to hit the road.'

Zac paid the bill, then caught hold of her hand as they walked to where he'd parked the car.

'Thanks for breakfast.'

He slanted her a warm smile. 'My pleasure.' As the night had been. And the early hours of the morning.

She made it easy for him to relax and unwind, didn't make any demands, and rarely rose to anger. None of which were an act. He never felt the need to play a part, and her wit and wisdom provided a lightness that had been seriously missing before she entered his life.

They reached the Jaguar, and he saw her into the passenger seat before crossing to the driver's side.

A few minutes, maybe five, was all it took to reach the street where her cottage was situated, and Lisane leant towards him as soon as he brought the car to a halt outside her gate.

'Take care, and don't work too hard.' She brushed her lips to his cheek, and bit back a faint gasp as he framed her face with his hands and took possession of her mouth.

Oh, my.

She could hardly find her breath when he released her, and she met his warm, steady gaze, glimpsed the faint wickedness evident…and wrinkled her nose at him in teasing remonstrance.

'I guess that'll hold me for a while.'

A wide smile curved his generous mouth. 'Sassy. Definitely sassy.'

Lisane reached for the door-clasp, caught up her overnight bag and slid out from the car. 'Go suss out the legal arguments that'll tie the bad guy up in legal knots.'

His soft laughter remained with her as the car disappeared from view, and she smiled a little as she extracted her house-key and unlocked the front door.

The morning was spent on household chores, and clearing the detritus of a hectic week. Wielding a very careful paintbrush, she completed the finishing touches to the remaining windowsills and two architraves.

Strong paint fumes provided a reason to escape the house for an hour or two, and she took the car to the nearest supermarket and stocked up on essential groceries. On her return she swiftly changed into old jeans and top, and spent time tending her garden. It wasn't a chore, for she loved the smell of freshly-turned soil, the caring work that produced a fine vegetable patch, the neatly trimmed ornamental shrubbery, and her pride...several herbs in terracotta pots.

Lisane liked to cook, and her kitchen bore all the necessary utensils needed for almost every dish in her late mother's repertoire of fine cuisine.

Who would have thought such a serious law student would thrive on domesticity? Or choose an aged, rundown cottage instead of high-rise apartment-living?

It probably had everything to do with her inherited French gene pool, she mused as she showered and washed her hair before pulling on shorts and a fresh top, then fixing an omelette stuffed with mushrooms, chives and a hint of garlic for her evening meal.

Afterwards she slotted in a DVD, watched it to the end, then climbed into bed and fell asleep within minutes of her head touching the pillow.

Sunday morning was divided between the gym, fixing decorative borders on the walls in the guest bedroom, then adding the white embroidered bedcover with its numerous ruffles and matching pillow covers.

It looked great, the numerous sewing hours necessary in its making well worthwhile.

Initially, she'd made allowances to cover tradesmen's expenses, for, although she could take care of the painting and most of the finishing touches, the kitchen had been in serious need of a complete overhaul and the acquisition of new electrical appliances. The bathroom and laundry also required new fittings. Electrical wiring replaced, the plumbing checked...

In many ways, it had been a mission. But now, twelve months down the track, she could honestly say she was pleased with the result, aware that the money spent had added measurably to the property's market value.

Lisane spent the afternoon completing the remaining architraves, then she cleaned up, took her laptop out to the small table and chair set beneath a magnificent jacaranda tree and caught up on work she needed to review in preparation for the following day.

Dinner was a mixed salad and smoked salmon, a bowl of fresh fruit, and she had just finished dispensing with the dishes when her cellphone rang.

She quickly dried her hands and picked up.

'Lisane…Solene.'

It wasn't seven already, surely? 'I was going to call you.' A quick glance at her watch assured it was a few minutes past the hour. 'How are all the wedding preparations?'

Her sister gave a faintly hollow laugh. 'We're contemplating an elopement.'

Lisane crossed into the lounge and sank into a comfortable chair. 'That bad, hmm?'

'Like you wouldn't believe.'

It didn't take three guesses to determine the source. 'Jean-Claude's beloved *maman*?'

'Uh-huh. Two weeks before the wedding she wants to change floral arrangements for the church…again.'

Two months ago it had been orchids, only to be discarded last month for cream roses.

'It gets worse,' Solene lamented. 'She thinks ivory would complement my gown, rather than pale pink, for the flower-girl, when the dressmaker has already finished the dress.' Solene gave a heartfelt groan in despair. 'I'm about ready to scream.'

Oh, dear. 'You've tried diplomacy?'

A significantly eloquent sigh echoed down the line. 'Been there, done that.'

Jean-Claude's mother had taken both Lisane and Solene beneath her maternal wing when they lost their own mother a few years ago, wistfully looking upon them as the daughters she'd never had. A kindly woman, with good intentions. Except for one slight flaw…she liked to be in control.

'It's your wedding,' Lisane pointed out gently.

'Hah!'

'Jean-Claude—'

'Issued an ultimatum this afternoon.'

'And?'

There was a few seconds' silence. 'Tears, apologies, more tears.'

She could imagine just how it went, and how distressed her sister had been. Wedding preparations should be pleasurable and exciting…not fraught with nervous tension.

'Two more weeks, Solene, then you can relax.'

'You think?'

'Definitely.'

'Your dress is gorgeous.'

They'd shared images via email, decided on colour, and as they were the same height and dress size it had been a simple matter for Solene to take Lisane's place with fittings.

'Can't wait to see you.'

Solene's faintly wistful response brought a slight lump to Lisane's throat. 'Me, too.' Weekly phone calls and email contact didn't cut it. 'Saturday.' She relayed her flight details, then ended the call.

* * *

Monday soon proved to be one of those days when whatever could go wrong…*did.*

Lisane woke late, saw the red digits blinking on her digital alarm, cursed the electrical fault through the night and hit the floor running to complete the fastest shower on record. Once dressed, she filched a cereal bar from its packet, collected her briefcase, laptop, and unlocked her garage.

She could still make it into the city on time *if* the traffic flow was unhindered by roadworks…

Lisane slid in behind the wheel of her VW Golf, ignited the engine, reversed out onto the street, navigated it, only to groan out loud minutes later as she saw the long stream of vehicles stretching as far as the eye could see.

When at last the endless convoy began to inch forward, no one seemed inclined to allow her to ease into the flow of traffic. Desperate measures were called for, and minutes later she made it amidst a cacophony of irate car horns accompanied by a few graphic hand gestures and mouthed blasphemy.

Why would the city council choose peak-hour traffic to conduct road repairs? Although, to be fair, this particular stretch bore heavy traffic all through the day and into the night.

She extracted her cellphone, activated the loudspeaker function and called work, notified her superior she'd be late, then continued the crawl-like pace into the central city.

Arriving late involved some serious catch-up time, and she examined the day's agenda, liaised with the police prosecutor, went through case notes, consulted with her client prior to his appearance in court—and, despite her cleverly structured questioning of the witness, the magistrate deemed in conclusion that there was sufficient evidence for the case to be heard in a higher court before a judge and jury at a future date.

It wasn't the result her client had hoped for, but, given his prior conviction and the strength of the witness's testimony, she could only reiterate fact and arrange a debriefing consultation.

Lunch was a chicken and salad sandwich followed by fresh fruit eaten at her desk, after which she made several phone calls and outlined pertinent points on her case notes prior to a late-afternoon consultation with a solicitor and his client, involving documented injuries incurred in an accident, which should conclude in a reasonable financial settlement for the client.

It was after five when Lisane saved all data to disk, closed down her laptop and pushed paperwork into her briefcase.

Home sounded good. She'd shower, don comfortable clothes, eat, then put in a few hours reviewing documentation in regard to a consultation scheduled for the following day.

An hour later she checked the contents of her refrigerator, decided she wasn't in the mood for food just yet and crossed to the small second bedroom which housed a desk, bookshelves filled with law books, her sewing machine and a dressmaker's dummy bedecked in a partly finished gown.

She could already 'see' the completed garment, the total picture with stiletto heels and evening bag, and her fingers began to itch as she viewed the soft drape of silk chiffon.

It wouldn't take much…

Within minutes she was attaching the requisite tacking, and she soon became lost to everything but the artistry of creation as she fed the chiffon carefully through the machine.

The thin spaghetti straps required a steady hand, and she measured the length, then fitted both.

There was immense satisfaction in the knowledge that only the fine hand-stitching remained, and she switched off the machine then stretched her arms high to ease the slight kink in her shoulders.

Food seemed a sensible option, and she fixed a tuna salad, filched bottled water from the refrigerator and ate while scanning the day's newspaper headlines.

It was after nine when she opened her briefcase and began reading documentation.

At some stage the burr of her cellphone intruded, and she picked up to discover Zac on the line.

'Hi.'

His soft chuckle curled round her nerve-ends and tugged a little. 'You sound distracted. Bad day?'

'It could have been better.'

There was a slight pause. 'Want to talk about it?'

What was the point? 'Not really.'

She could almost see the way his deep brown eyes darkened, the hard acceptance beneath a degree of cynicism. Criminal law dealt on occasion with the underbelly of society, people who possessed few if any scruples and some who committed unspeakable acts.

'All we can do is our best.'

Lisane gave a slight grimace. 'And when the best isn't good enough?'

'For whom? The client whose prior record makes him a threat to the community?'

It wasn't about winning, but representing the law within the parameters of a legal system designed to seek justice for all.

Her lips curved into a faint smile. 'OK, now you've made me feel better…how was your day?'

'I could come tell you in person.'

She was tempted. Seriously tempted. Terrific sex, and afterwards strong, warm arms to cradle her close. For a moment the image was overwhelming, and she queried lightly, 'Are you waiting for an invitation?'

'No.'

A bubble of laughter escaped her throat at the faint mockery in his voice, and she voiced teasingly, 'See you in fifteen.'

Fourteen, Lisane determined as headlights threw a sweeping beam across the front of her cottage, followed seconds later by the faint snick of a car door closing.

Lisane met him on the front porch, her eyes wide and faintly luminous in the dimmed light as he framed her face.

His mouth brushed hers, felt her lips part in welcome, and he angled his head and went in deep, savouring the taste and the scent of her. Wanting, needing her warmth, her touch.

Dammit, all of her.

He was aware of her arms reaching to encircle his neck, and felt her fingers weave into the thickness of his hair, sensed their soothing movement against his scalp and he feathered a light path down the length of her spine to cup her bottom, bringing her against the thick hardness of his desire.

He could take her now, dispense with her clothes, his

own…the effect she had on him was a sorcery both sweet and carnal.

For a moment he'd neglected to remember where they were, clearly visible in the dim porch light to anyone who chanced a look.

Zac eased back a little, and reluctantly relinquished her mouth as he leant his forehead against her own.

She was incapable of saying a word as he shaped her shoulders, then he let his hands slide down her arms to thread his fingers through her own.

'Let's take this indoors, hmm?'

The cottage design was simple. A wide hallway separated the lounge on one side from the main bedroom opposite. From there the hallway opened into a large living area, with two small bedrooms to the left. The kitchen, bathroom and utility room stretched across the rear of the cottage.

Silently she turned at his direction and together they entered the hallway and closed the door behind them.

Zac lifted a hand and trailed fingers down her cheek. 'Are you done with work for the night?'

It would be easy to say *yes*, only for honesty to win out. 'Not quite.'

His thumb pressed against the centre of her lower lip, and his smile held a tinge of amusement as he released her. 'I'll go make coffee.'

Lisane watched him turn towards the kitchen, and she let her gaze linger on the wide expanse of shoulder, aware of the powerful musculature beneath the fine chambray shirt. The taut waist and the tight butt moulded by figure-fitting black jeans.

Just looking at him made her heart rhythm accelerate

to a faster beat. And that was only part of it! Her nerves flared and took on a life of their own, almost *humming* with the anticipation of his touch…his possession.

To be so attuned to him scared her a little. It was as if he was a part of her, attached but not bound.

There were times when she could tell what he was thinking, predict how he would react in a given situation.

Then just as she thought she could read him, he would surprise her…as he did now.

Coffee?

He'd disappear calmly into the kitchen and do coffee, when she could have sworn he'd sweep an arm beneath her knees and carry her into the bedroom?

Sure, she could follow him, wind her arms round his neck, pull his face down to hers…and invite him to continue from where he'd left off.

It was what she *wanted* to do.

Instead she settled down, found her place in the documentation and continued reading, pausing occasionally to make notes.

Minutes later Zac placed a mug of steaming coffee on the desk, then he crossed to the bookcase, retrieved a book and trailed light fingers across her shoulders.

'I'll take this into the lounge. Join me when you're done.'

Lisane lifted her head, caught his warm smile…and felt her bones begin to melt.

The anticipation, the promise of how the evening would end, sent heat curling deep in her belly, and a faint tinge of pink coloured her cheeks as she caught the teasing quality evident in his dark gaze.

'Go,' she directed with mock severity, and heard his husky chuckle as he left the room.

Dammit, how could she possibly focus on *work* when all she could think of was *him*?

Fifteen minutes later she closed the bulky file and slid it into her briefcase. Then she stood, stretched her arms high in order to ease the faint kink at the base of her neck, collected her empty coffee mug and returned it to the kitchen before entering the lounge.

Zac looked up, closed the book he'd been reading and extended his hand without offering so much as a word.

Lisane crossed to his side and let him pull her down onto his lap.

His hand shaped the back of her head as he eased her cheek into the curve of his shoulder. 'Tired?'

It was so good to feel the solid thud of his heart and have his fingers begin a soothing massage at her nape.

Restful…not. How could she relax when her entire body was incredibly attuned to *his*?

The exclusive subtle scent of his aftershave teased her senses, as did the clean smell of his skin, his clothes. But it was more than the shape and form of him. She admired his sharp mind and his degree of integrity, adored his sense of humour and his ability to relax away from the strictures of his profession.

Yet on another level his legal expertise in the court-room held her in awe, exposing as it did a steel-like ruthlessness that showed no mercy. A quality that put him ahead of his contemporaries and earned immeasurable respect.

A man one coveted as a friend, and had every reason to fear as an enemy.

'Difficult case?'

Lisane lifted her head and met eyes that were dark and slumberous. 'Just a lot of information to absorb.'

Zac inclined his head in agreement. 'In order to cover any unexpected contingencies.'

Even in the most open-and-closed case, one needed to be prepared for the element of surprise by opposing counsel.

'Anything you want to run by me?'

One minor detail kept sticking in her mind, and she voiced it, instinct rather than purported fact providing the slight niggle of disquiet.

She knew all the angles, and had explored each and every one of them, consulted her superior...yet still it refused to gel.

'Instinct should never be ignored.' Zac's eyes narrowed slightly. 'Where are you tempted to go with this?'

It sounded illogical, even as she relayed her thoughts, yet his slight indication of agreement gave a sense of satisfaction.

'It's possible.'

Lisane examined his features carefully. 'But not probable.'

'Always be prepared to expect the unexpected.'

It was a mantra every law student learnt by heart, and she gave him a lopsided smile. 'Point taken.'

His fingers threaded through the silky length of her hair, shaped her head and brought it close to his own.

The touch of his mouth was warm against her softly parted lips, and she was unable to prevent a husky murmur of approval as he slipped a hand beneath the hem of her T-shirt and sought a silk-encased breast, teasing the firm flesh as he unerringly found its hardening peak.

His mouth firmed over hers, taking her deep as his tongue tangled with her own, seeking to conquer in a manner that tore the breath from her throat.

Lisane wound her arms around his neck and held on, savouring his touch, his possession, as she met and matched his own.

There was no sense of time or place. Only the desire to assuage a mutual need.

His clothes, hers, became a frustrating irritation and she didn't protest as he tugged her T-shirt over her head, then freed the clasp on her bra.

Her hands were equally busy as she undid the buttons on his shirt, then reached for the fastener on his jeans.

With one fluid movement Zac rose to his feet with her in his arms, heard her bubbling laughter, stilled it with his mouth, and carried her through to the main bedroom.

'Witch.' The huskily voiced imprecation held amused resignation as he tumbled them both down onto her bed.

'And that makes you…what?' she teased, then gasped as he removed his jeans, shucked off his briefs and dispensed with the remainder of her clothing.

'Let's find out, shall we?'

His erection was a potent force, and she soothed the silky head with an exploratory touch, heard the breath hiss through his teeth, then she brushed the taut skin with a few finger-pads, lightly, in a deliberate tease that brought a husky groan from his lips.

Control…he had it. Yet she was fascinated to discover what it would take to break it.

How far would he allow her to go?

Seconds later it was her turn to gasp as he sought the satiny folds at the entrance to her femininity and latched on to the highly sensitised nub, initiating a deliberate stroking movement that sent her wild.

Soon it wasn't enough, and she was barely aware of

urging his possession as sensation spiralled, sending her high...so high it was almost more than she could bear.

'Now.' Was that her voice *begging* for release? The part of her brain that engaged rationale insisted it had to be.

'Not yet.'

Oh, dear heaven. *Yes*. Otherwise she'd go insane with need.

Except he wasn't done. And she almost wept as he brought her to fever pitch...with his hands, his mouth in an oral supplication that blew her away, so far out of her mind she barely stifled an exultant scream as he entered her in one powerful thrust.

Her vaginal muscles contracted, tightly sheathing him as she stretched to accommodate him. When he began to move, she met and matched his rhythm as shameless, pulsating emotion took them to an electrifying high, held them there, then tipped them over into a magically sensual nirvana that was erotic and exquisitely primitive.

Treacherous, Lisane reflected later as she lay in Zac's arms on the edge of sleep.

Because she never wanted it to end.

An inner voice silently demanded, 'Does it have to?'

Sadly, she didn't have an answer.

CHAPTER THREE

THE day's workload commanded all of Lisane's attention, and it was mid-afternoon before news of a colleague's promotion reached her ears.

Well-deserved, given Sue's attention to detail and unrelenting dedication to each case she handled.

'Celebration time. Champagne on me. Tomorrow night?' came through via inter-office email, and over the next hour responses indicated a resounding 'yes', followed by Sue's instructions re time and place.

The thought of a girls' night out was a pleasurable one, and Lisane spent Tuesday evening making notations from various law books. Gradually, with steady persistence, she was gathering sufficient information to present a strong case. Together with covering every contingency opposing counsel might draw from.

Even so, there was that edge, the knowledge she may have slipped up on one unexpected but important detail.

It kept her up late, and resulted in pertinent dialogue with her superior next day.

Consequently it was a relief to slip behind the wheel of her car and juggle peak hour traffic clogging the arterial roads leading from the city.

She reached the cottage with an hour in which to shower, dress and be on the road again.

Basic black was 'go anywhere' attire, and Lisane fixed her hair into a careless knot, applied blusher and lipgloss, then slid her feet into stilettos, collected her purse, her keys, and locked the front door before slipping in behind the wheel of her silver Golf.

Traffic flow into the city was steady, and she parked beneath the inner-city hotel, then took the lift up to the Atrium lounge.

Three of her associates were comfortably settled with drinks before them, and no sooner had Lisane greeted them than the final member of their coterie arrived.

It was lovely to relax and unwind away from the office. To talk without the constant constraints of work, and they took their time before crossing into the restaurant.

Champagne was the celebratory toast of choice, and Sue's promotion was given due merit before a waiter delivered their starters.

Fine food and drink, and good company. Who could ask for anything more of an evening spent with friends?

The amazing thing in being the fabulous five, as they regarded themselves, was the friendship they shared in and out of the office. There was no element of envy, jealousy or the desire for one-upmanship…just five young women who got along.

'Oh, my. Look who's just walked in.'

Someone of note, obviously, Lisane deduced as she discreetly turned her head, only to feel her stomach twist at the sight of Allegra in the company of her parents.

Dressed to kill in a red cut-away cocktail gown that ventured into the almost-too-much-skin territory, Allegra resembled a catwalk model…confident, faintly aloof, and stunning.

'Wow.'

Sue's hushed comment didn't come close, and the questions followed in tandem.

'No male partner?'

'Maybe he's joining them?'

'The question is…*who*?'

Speculative conjecture at its best…and discretion, given it was no secret Allegra had her eye on Zac Winstone.

More than an eye, Lisane accorded silently. The female barrister was in for the kill, and didn't care who knew it!

'Uh-oh, she's just picked up her cellphone.'

'She's smiling.'

'The woman's a bitch. In and out of the courtroom.'

'OK, girls, let's move it along, shall we?'

Sue lifted her champagne flute. 'Sure. Here's to women doing it for themselves.'

'Ah…you might like to rephrase that.'

Amelie grinned. 'Just checking you're on the ball.'

'Wicked.'

'But fun.'

Truly a girls' night out, Lisane decided with a degree of humour. Memorable, in that their jobs dealt with serious issues within the parameters of the law. Where evil intent superceded good, and justice needed to be seen to be done. Not always successfully.

Making it work was the challenge. Examining legal precedents in order to close any slight loopholes opposing counsel might offer. And above all, attempting to do one's best for the client…whether guilty or innocent.

'What are your thoughts on the Marshall case?'

There was a collective groan. 'Forbidden territory. Nothing, but *nothing* to do with work is going to escape our lips tonight.'

There was a pause while the waiter delivered their mains, and Sue barely waited until he was out of earshot before voicing,

'OK, so let's have an update on the men in our lives.'

The theme was familiar, Lisane mused. Lack of dedication to the relationship, little if any commitment, and emphasis on sex. Two young women in their group were content with the status quo, while one appeared misty-eyed and vowed she wanted the ring, marriage and family.

'Lisane?'

'Pass.'

'Not good enough. Answer the question.' Sue's teasing mockery brought some light laughter, and Lisane entered into the spirit of the game.

'Sorry, counsellor. Privileged information.'

'Damn.'

'Don't look, but a serious hunk of a guy is being led towards Allegra's table.'

Lisane controlled the desire to check. Common sense reassured her that it couldn't be Zac. But just for a few seconds the possibility didn't seem beyond the realm of reality. The Winstone and Fabrisi families were legal and social equals, dedicated to charitable causes, and were frequently seen in each other's company.

Surely Zac would have told her if he intended to join Allegra and her parents this evening…wouldn't he?

Allegra had developed manipulation into an art form, and possessed few, if any, scruples where Zac was concerned.

'Wonder who he is?'

'Family friend?' Sue ventured. 'The parents are greeting him like a long-lost son.'

The waiter cleared their plates and took an order for dessert…sinful choices in the name of celebration, and warranting some serious time in the gym to compensate.

Coffee followed, and they lingered a while, then took care of the bill and made their way to the powder-room.

Lisane was the last to leave, and just as she opened the door it swung in, causing a hasty few steps back to avoid a collision.

The last person she wanted to see up close was Allegra…but there was no avoiding a confrontation. One Lisane opted to make very brief.

'Allegra.'

'He's my cousin, darling.' Words spoken without preamble, and the woman's smile held a brilliance that was totally at variance with the cool glitter in her eyes. 'On a brief visit from Perth.'

'How nice for you.' She stepped around Allegra in a bid to leave the powder-room, only to have her passage blocked.

'He's serious eye-candy, and does service as a social handbag.'

Lisane held the young woman's gaze and successfully masked her disquiet. 'My friends are waiting for me.'

'Another minute or two won't matter.' Allegra smoothed a hand over one slender hip, then she speared a lacquered nail in the air a few inches from Lisane's face. 'Take note. Zac is mine.'

It took two to fight, and she wasn't about to go there. 'If that's true,' she managed evenly, 'why is he with me?'

Allegra's eyes became ice. 'You must know Zac will never marry you.'

She needed an exit line, fast! 'Did it occur to you we might be content with the relationship,' she waited a deliberate beat, then added quietly, 'the way it is?'

'Not for long.' The woman's triumph was tainted with evil satisfaction. 'Any time soon his ring will be on my finger.'

'Really?' How could she sound so calm, when inside her nerves were shredding? She held Allegra's gaze as she took a determined step forward, silently challenging the woman to step aside.

For a moment it didn't appear as if Allegra was going to move, then she lifted one eyebrow in a gesture of disdain and shifted slightly.

Lisane stilled the urge to rush out the door, choosing a measured, unhurried pace, and braced her shoulders against the nervous tension feathering icily down her spine.

'We were about to initiate a rescue mission,' Sue declared quietly as Lisane joined the group of four young women lingering a few feet distant. 'Are you OK?'

'Fine.' She managed a warm smile. 'Let's go, shall we?'

It wasn't difficult to keep up a carefree façade as they took the lift down to the car park, and she kept the smile in place until she slid in behind the wheel of her car.

Allegra's taunts echoed inside her head, and she almost wished she'd told the woman to get a life...except common sense had silently warned of the possibility of professional repercussions.

Allegra Fabrisi held a degree of power...a word here and there, an unfair criticism, and it could result in the speculative attention of Lisane's peers.

Roll on Saturday!

Three weeks' absence in Sydney would provide a welcome breathing space. There were the final planning stages, the wedding itself and a lovely break in which to visit the beach, check out the shopping malls, and just relax.

Lisane collected the sack of groceries from the seat of her car and carried them indoors.

The dinner menu she'd planned for Friday evening was relatively simple, and she toed off her stilettos, then quickly assembled ingredients and began preparations.

An evening meal timed for seven enabled her to cook, then shower and change and set the table.

She made it with a few minutes to spare, and she slid the herb bread into the oven as the doorbell rang.

Zac's familiar tall frame filled the aperture, and the mere sight of him sent the beat of her heart into overdrive.

'Hi.'

He'd discarded a professional business suit for black tailored trousers, a white chambray collarless shirt and a black butter-soft leather jacket.

Wow seemed an inadequate description.

'Come through,' she managed steadily, and she stood aside so he could precede her down the hallway.

With considerable ease he paused to drop an overnight bag in her bedroom, shrugged out of his jacket, then he gathered her in against him and took possession of her mouth in a leisurely kiss.

Oh, my, was all she could think when he released her.

He'd brought wine, which he took into the kitchen, uncorked and let breathe while he admired the finishing touches she'd made to the room.

'Would you like a drink?'

Zac turned towards her. 'Just wine with dinner.'

Lisane checked the herb bread, saw it was beginning to crisp, and enquired about his day.

'Fact-gathering, validating authenticity, a conference call.' And one intriguing brief he had yet to decide whether to accept. 'You?'

'Nothing out of the ordinary.' Just a pile of paperwork she'd needed to shift before day's end, notations for ongoing cases ensuring the colleague taking over her workload for the next three weeks was *au fait* with current files.

Last night she'd packed her bag ready for the flight to Sydney. As bridesmaid, she'd also assembled games and prizes for Solene's bridal shower party, and the hen-party. All she needed to do in the morning was add last-minute essentials before Zac drove her to the airport.

The food with its delicate sauce was a hit, and she took pleasure in Zac's compliment.

She was far from a domestic goddess, but she liked making her home attractive, cooking good food and presenting it well. It seemed to be a family trait, for Solene read cookbooks as others read…books.

Dessert comprised a fresh fruit salad jazzed up with wine and accompanied by whipped cream drizzled with crystallized sugar, and afterwards they took coffee in the lounge.

It was comfortable having him here like this. Her territory, with its easy familiarity.

She was going to miss him, miss *this*, being with him, sleeping with him…forget the *sleep* part, making love with him.

For her it was *love*, not simply the act of sharing physical sex. Had he guessed how it was for her? In a way she hoped not, for it would only increase her vulnerability level.

Tonight was special. She'd set the scene with fine food, and soon…soon he'd take her hand and lead the way to her bedroom.

It was there they'd indulge all the senses, and make love long into the night. Her imagination took flight, creating images which heated the blood and set her pulse racing to an increased beat, until the wanting became need.

He knew. Had to, and the warmth of his smile held sensual promise as he rose to his feet.

His kiss possessed warmth, then heat, and she leant into him, absorbing his strength as she kissed him back with hungry passion.

A hunger Zac returned in kind as they moved towards the bedroom, shedding clothes along the way.

Naked, he cupped her bottom and lifted her high against him, then he lowered his head and took the peak of her breast into his mouth, nipping the hardened aureole with his teeth until she reached the brink between pleasure and pain.

Lisane retaliated with a love bite to the sensitive curve at the edge of his neck, felt his body tense, then he shifted his attention to her mouth in a possession that shredded every nerve-cell in her body.

Just as she thought she might need to communicate a need to breathe, he positioned her to accept his hardened length and surged into her moist heat, filling her as he released her mouth and buried his lips in the hollow at the base of her throat.

She was with him, part of him, body and soul, and she began to move, slowly at first, then with increasing abandon until she became almost a wild thing in his arms.

It wasn't enough, for there was so much more, and together they fell onto the bed in a tangle of limbs and laughter, to love each other again and again through the night until exhaustion overcame passion and they drifted to sleep in each other's arms.

The alarm sounded loud, too loud, and Lisane groaned, hit the *off* button, glimpsed at the darkened room and buried her head beneath the pillow.

It couldn't be five already.

'One hour to check-in time,' Zac drawled as he reached for the bedside lamp. 'Shower, dress, coffee, then hit the road.'

How much sleep had she had?

Not enough, she decided as a hand whipped away the pillow and tossed back the bedcovers.

'OK, OK,' she muttered. 'I'm out of here.'

The shower did much to waken her, and Zac's presence in the shower stall ensured she didn't linger over-long… although the temptation to savour his tautly muscled body was hard to resist.

Except it wasn't an option, given the time constraint, and almost as if he knew he took possession of her mouth in a brief, hard kiss, then released her.

'Go,' he said huskily. 'Or you won't make the flight.'

It took only minutes to towel herself dry, then she pulled on a robe and made for the kitchen, where the aroma of freshly brewed coffee greeted her.

She filled two mugs, added sugar, then sipped hers with

appreciation. It was hot, too hot, and she decided to dress while it cooled.

Zac was in the process of dressing when she entered the bedroom. She quickly collected fresh underwear, donned it, then pulled on jeans, a cotton top, stepped into jogging shoes and applied minimum make-up, fixed her hair, then she shrugged into a tailored jacket, placed toiletries and make-up into her bag and fastened it. All done.

They had a smooth run through to the airport, and Lisane checked in her bag as a voice on the Tannoy announced last call for boarding on her flight.

It was better this way, she decided as Zac caught her close for a brief hard kiss. Then she went through the security barrier, turning briefly to wave at him before disappearing down the long passageway leading to her flight departure bay.

Three weeks was a long time. Too long, she despaired, equally torn between wanting to stay and needing to leave.

Although she'd get to see him next weekend when he flew in for Solene's wedding.

The one-hour forty-minute flight was uneventful, except there was the familiar pull of *home* as she caught sight of Sydney Harbour, the famed bridge and nearby opera house.

Disembarking was achieved with minimum ease, and there, waiting just inside the Arrivals lounge, were her sister and fiancé.

Hugs, laughter, and more hugs as they greeted each other before lining up at the luggage carousel.

There was so much to say, such excitement, that Lisane and Solene barely drew breath during the drive to suburban Manly on the northern side of the city.

Daylight saving had not long come into effect, which meant Sydney time was an hour ahead of Brisbane.

'All the girls will be here around two for the bridal shower.'

Hadn't she checked the list, in-flight, that Solene had emailed detailing the lead-up to the wedding?

Saturday afternoon, bridal shower.

Sunday, barbecue with Jean-Claude's parents.

Monday, dress fittings.

Tuesday, last-minute shopping.

Wednesday…what was Wednesday?

Thursday, wedding rehearsal.

Friday, collect all wedding gear and run a final check of everything.

As the bride's sister and only bridesmaid, Lisane was in charge of ensuring everything ran as smoothly as possible.

A priority was to unpack and change, eat lunch on the run while checking there was sufficient food and drink for the afternoon, the novelty games she'd organised as entertainment, gift prizes…and text-message Zac.

Jean Claude left minutes before the first guest arrived, and it became a fun-filled few hours with some twenty young women and Jean-Claude's mother present.

There was some teasing and much laughter as Solene received some lovely gifts, and Jean-Claude's mother lingered to help clean up after the last guest departed.

'Alain is so looking forward to seeing you again,' Chantelle confided. 'He's been at a bit of a loss since you moved away to Brisbane.'

She gave Chantelle a warm hug. 'It'll be lovely to catch up with you all. How is Henri?'

'He's well, dear. I'm hoping you and Alain will spend some time together.'

Lisane felt an edge of tension begin to make itself known. Alain was the youngest son, and perhaps his mother's favoured son…one she had so hoped Lisane would marry.

'I have a partner,' she said gently, aware Chantelle knew of Zac's existence in her life. 'You'll meet him when he flies in for the wedding.'

'Yes, but you're not engaged or committed to him, are you?'

There was no sting intended in the words, and none taken, but they served to remind her neither Chantelle nor Alain had accepted she'd moved on.

'Sorry,' Solene intimated after Chantelle left. 'I meant to warn you.'

'It's OK.' What else could she say?

Dinner was a convivial meal, and afterwards they spent time reviewing the guest list, the table seating at the reception venue, then clarified a few minor details Solene wanted Lisane to check, so it was late when they decided to head to bed.

'Tomorrow,' Solene bade with a weary smile, 'we talk about *you*. I want to hear first-hand all about the hunk in your life.'

What to tell? Lisane contemplated over breakfast next morning when her sister quizzed her about Zac.

'He's special.' And how!

'You love him.' It was a statement, not a query, and one she couldn't deny.

'Does he love you?' Solene persisted gently as she refreshed their tea and coffee.

Did he? She couldn't be sure. Affection, without doubt, and passion. Or was it merely lust? 'I hope so.'

'Has he asked you to move in with him?'

Sleeping over wasn't the same as living together. Would she, if he asked her? In a heartbeat. 'We prefer our independence.'

'Darling, this is Solene, your sister, remember? We don't keep secrets from each other.'

A soul-searching heart-to-heart? 'He hasn't asked,' she responded lightly. 'But if he did, the answer is yes.'

The phone rang, and Solene took the call…which successfully diverted the conversation.

'Chantelle,' Solene informed, 'suggesting we go over before the guests arrive this afternoon for some family time. Apparently she's planned a surprise.'

And what a surprise it turned out to be!

Stretched high beneath Jean-Claude's parents' covered terrace was a banner proclaiming 'Welcome home, Lisane!'

There were hugs and kisses, a celebratory cake…and Alain.

Lisane didn't know whether to laugh or cry, and somehow managed both…but not for the reasons Chantelle, Henri or Alain imagined.

Accept it in the spirit in which it's meant, she thought, and she did, joining in the gaiety with spontaneous enjoyment.

Alain, however, was something else.

He was a friend, a good one of long standing. But that was all. Throughout the afternoon she endeavoured to indicate that, except he chose not to notice.

Wherever she moved, he ensured he was not far from her side. He'd touch her arm, put a light arm loosely over her shoulder. Top up her drink, check she had sufficient to eat.

To everyone else it appeared to be simple friendship, but she knew she wasn't mistaken in thinking that, as far as Alain was concerned, there was more to it than that. And there wasn't much she could do about it.

At least, not here, not now.

The last thing she wanted to do was hurt his feelings, or upset Chantelle.

There was an awkward moment when her cellphone rang and she took a call from Zac, choosing to move indoors for a degree of privacy.

The sound of his voice curled through her body and made the blood in her veins sing.

'Working hard?' she managed lightly, aware he was deep in preparations for a case due to begin in court the next day.

'Taking a break. And you?'

'Attending a barbecue hosted by Jean-Claude's parents.'

'Have fun.'

Wish you were here. 'Will do. I'll text-message you tomorrow.'

'Sleep well,' Zac bade, and ended the call.

Not without you, she added silently, longing for his touch, the feel of him beneath her hands, her lips.

When she re-emerged Alain caught hold of her hand, and brushed his lips to her temple. 'Please,' she protested quietly.

'I've missed you so much.'

'Nothing has changed, Alain. Don't do this.'

'Let me take you to dinner tomorrow night.'

'I'm sorry.' She gently disentangled her hand and mingled with the guests, helped Chantelle organised coffee, and afterwards joined her in the kitchen as they cleaned up.

It was after eleven when Solene and Jean-Claude indicated the need to leave, and Lisane gave a silent sigh of relief the evening had come to an end.

The following few days were hectic, with visits to the dressmaker for fittings, checking with the florist, the cake decorator, ensuring there were sufficient sugared almonds…and a moment of blind panic when Solene discovered there was a hitch with her specially designed wedding ring, and it would be a rush to have it finished on time.

Lisane calmed her sister down, spoke firmly with the jeweller…and repeated the process a day later when the wedding caterer enlightened them that the warehouse wouldn't be able to supply the exact napkins Solene had chosen for the tables.

Wednesday evening's hen-party provided some light relief, in that Lisane had chosen a theme and invited several of Solene's girlfriends to participate in the fun and games…all of which involved accentuating Solene's final few days as a single woman.

'If you've organised a male stripper, I'll kill you,' Solene vowed as Lisane announced the main event.

'Something infinitely more tasteful.'

Jean-Claude, disguised as a pirate, to spirit Solene away for the night. Except first he had a part to play…which he did very well, and it was only when Solene began to yell for help that he revealed his identity. After which he scooped his wife-to-be into his arms and carried her out to the waiting limousine, whose trunk held a bag with a change of clothes.

The most solemn pre-wedding event was the wedding rehearsal, scheduled for Thursday evening at the church.

Jean-Claude had chosen Alain to be his best man, which meant Lisane, as bridesmaid, would be his partner for the day and the official part of the evening.

The immediate family gathered and went through their practised steps without a hitch at the minister's direction.

Afterwards they all went on to a restaurant to celebrate the rehearsal in anticipation of the day itself.

Two evenings from now Solene and Jean-Claude would be married, the wedding party would be in full swing... with Zac at Lisane's side.

She was almost counting the hours!

CHAPTER FOUR

SATURDAY dawned bright and clear, with the promise of mild early-summer sunshine. Tree leaves glistened with droplets of moisture from an overnight rain-shower, and there was a freshness in the air that boded well for a lovely day.

In keeping with tradition Jean-Claude had spent the night at his parents' home, and Lisane slipped a robe over her nightshirt and padded into the kitchen.

Ten minutes later she knocked on Solene's bedroom door and placed the tray of food she'd prepared on the bedside pedestal.

'I smell coffee.'

'Breakfast,' Lisane announced with a laughing smile as her sister slid up in the bed and sleepily examined the tray.

Juice, eggs benedict, bacon, croissants, jam, and steaming black coffee.

'Yum.'

'There's enough for two.' She sank down onto the edge of the bed, picked up a hot, crisp croissant, then bit into it with a blissful expression.

'This is the bride and bridesmaid thing?'

Lisane took another bite. 'Sisterly.' She motioned to

the tray. 'Eat up. From here on in the day is going to be a hectic rush.'

'So says the bridesmaid—'

'Who's been a bridesmaid or three, and knows the score.'

Solene sipped her juice and wrinkled her nose. 'Is this the part where we discuss vitally important things like—?'

'The birds and the bees, and preparing oneself for the new husband?' she queried, tongue-in-cheek, and watched her sister break into unrestrained laughter.

'A bit late for that, isn't it?'

'Well,' Lisane said primly. 'I aim to do my best.'

'Thanks,' Solene said gently. 'I'm so glad you're here to share the day with me. It wouldn't be the same without you.'

'Same goes.'

The eggs benedict were divine, even if she said so herself, and the coffee was to die for.

'The florist is delivering—'

'At nine,' Lisane reassured. 'Jean-Claude has the rings. Zac is taking a cab from the airport and should be here around eleven.'

'The photographer is due at one, Chantelle is dropping off Henri at two and taking Zac back to the house. He'll go to the church with Jean-Claude and Alain. The limousines are booked to arrive at two-thirty.'

Solene lifted a hand and Lisane gave it a high-five.

'Piece of cake.'

Well, almost.

The hairdresser was late…the result of a flat tyre. The make-up artist went to the right street in the wrong suburb and rang in a panic for directions.

'Tell me again,' Solene said in a controlled voice. 'This *is* supposed to be the happiest day of my life?'

Lisane attempted to soothe. 'Everything will be fine.'

'Hah!'

The phone rang for the umpteenth time, and Lisane took the call. It was Chantelle, concerned the flowers to decorate the church had yet to arrive.

Lisane sorted it out, relayed the florist's van was due any minute. The doorbell rang, and she let in the make-up artist.

A short while later she opened the door to find Zac standing in the aperture.

'Hi.'

He took in the silk robe, rollers in her hair, caught the slightly frazzled expression and reached for her, enjoying for a brief second the surprised look in her eyes before he captured her mouth in a slow-burning kiss that promised much.

When he lifted his head she could only look at him in total bemusement, and his lips curved into a warm smile.

'Better.'

'I have to…' She gestured helplessly towards the lounge, and he pressed a thumb-pad to her lips.

'I know.' He picked up a suit-bag and hooked it over one shoulder, then collected his overnight bag. 'Show me where to stow these. Then tell me what I can do.'

He followed her down the hallway and deposited his gear, then he cupped her head and kissed her again.

'Much better.'

He looked so good. Felt so good. It was so utterly tempting to move back into his arms.

Except there was a wedding to prepare for, a bride to calm, and they all needed to eat.

'Lunch,' Lisane offered, distracted. 'I made sandwiches early this morning. They're on platters in the refrigerator.'

She gestured in the general direction of the kitchen. 'I'll make coffee. Or there's bottled water—'

'Go.' Zac shrugged out of his jacket and tossed it on the bed. 'I'll take care of it.'

They took a fifteen-minute lunch break, and from then on in everything seemed to progress smoothly.

The make-up artist and the hairdresser worked in tandem, creating magic, then it was time to dress.

The photographer and his assistant arrived ahead of time, so too did Henri, courtesy of Chantelle, who collected Zac, and before long it was time to leave for the church.

Solene had chosen a simple gown in the palest silk chiffon *café au lait*, with a fitted strapless bodice and a full-length skirt that flared in soft folds from the hipline. Instead of a veil, she draped a long, soft scarf in matching silk chiffon over her hair. The effect was stunning, and in her hand she carried a beautiful budded red rose.

Lisane's gown was identical in style, in a deeper coffee colour.

'You make a beautiful bride.' Lisane gave Solene a careful hug. 'Love you heaps.'

'Thanks. You, too.' Solene blinked rapidly. 'Oh, hell, I wasn't going to do this.'

'No tears allowed.' She offered a soft grin. 'Think mascara and foundation touch-ups, arriving late at the church.'

Solene's lips trembled a little, then she turned towards Henri. 'Let's go do this, shall we?'

Jean-Claude's father took her arm and touched light fingers to Solene's cheek. 'It is a great honour to escort you into the care of my son.'

Lisane followed her sister to the limousine, ensuring her gown was safely tucked in before she left the chauffeur to close the door, then she slid into the second bridal car.

It was the most poignant wedding she'd attended, for many reasons, the foremost being Solene and Jean-Claude's obvious love for each other. There was a touch of sadness that her parents weren't able to witness the occasion, and an emotional few minutes when Solene and Jean-Claude said their personal vows.

Alain took his role as best man very seriously... although perhaps that should be amended to Alain enjoying his role as her partner a little too well.

Although why shouldn't he slip an arm around the back of her waist or take hold of her hand as they stood with Solene and Jean-Claude during the photographic session featuring family and guests?

The closeness was solely for the benefit of the photographer and the bridal photos. So why did she harbour an uncomfortable feeling Alain was silently staking a claim?

Was it because of Zac's presence among the guests?

Don't be silly, she silently chastised. She was just being acutely sensitive, and blamed the feeling on an over-active imagination.

Although the feeling increased as they joined Solene and Jean-Claude in the limousine, in which they were driven to a prearranged destination for bridal shots.

It was more than an hour before they returned to the reception venue, where the numerous guests mixed and mingled in the large lounge area. Waiters were in evidence offering trays of canapés and drinks.

Lisane skimmed the room, and saw Zac in conversation with Chantelle and Henri. Immaculately attired, he stood out from every other male among the fellow guests. It wasn't so much the cut of his clothes, but the man himself.

He gave the impression of being very relaxed and laid-back, but beneath the calm exterior was a razor-sharp mind and a compelling ability to analyse the minds of others. It made him a powerful adversary in the court-room, and a man only a fool would choose to cross.

She began weaving her way through the numerous guests, pausing every now and then to converse with a friend, an acquaintance.

'Ah, there you are,' Chantelle greeted with a smile. 'We were just explaining to Zac how Henri and I regard you as part of our family.'

'You've both been very kind,' Lisane said with genuine sincerity. 'Solene looked beautiful, don't you think?'

Zac reached for her hand and laced his fingers through her own, then brought them to his lips. 'So do you.' His eyes held hers, and she couldn't look away.

Oh, my. She could feel the heat flare deep inside and send tiny flames licking through her veins. There was the anticipation, the promise of how the night would end.

She was supremely conscious of him, the innate sensuality he managed to exude without any effort at all…and its effect.

His fingers tightened fractionally on hers, and it was all she could do to control the piercing sweetness suffusing her body.

Everything faded from the periphery of her vision, and for a moment she lost sight of time and place.

Almost as if he knew, he brushed a thumb-pad against the veins at her wrist, and she offered a slow smile that undoubtedly didn't fool him in the slightest.

'Ah, here's Alain.'

Lisane heard the relief evident in Chantelle's voice and turned slightly to accommodate his presence.

'The *maître d'* wants to seat the bridal party and begin serving the first course.'

Was there an element of disapproval in Alain's voice?

'Of course,' she said at once, and turned towards Zac. 'I won't have much of a chance to catch up with you until later.'

He trailed light fingers down her cheek. 'Enjoy.'

The food and champagne went down well…a little too well for Alain, and the toasts and speeches were given in an amusing vein, which brought laughter from the guests when Jean-Claude mentioned some of the highlights of courting Solene.

The cutting of the cake became a celebratory moment, and afterwards the DJ set up his equipment.

There were friends among the guests, people Lisane had known all her life. With Zac by her side, his hand linked with hers, it was almost possible to sense the silent conjecture his presence generated as she effected introductions.

'You're a hit, especially among the women,' Lisane declared with sparkling humour, and sensed his amusement.

'I'm duly flattered.'

The bridal waltz began and they watched Jean-Claude lead Solene onto the floor, then circle it to a slow, haunting waltz.

Alain crossed to her side and took her hand. 'We're next.'

Together they followed the bridal pair's lead, and were soon joined by Chantelle and Henri, then the majority of the guests.

'Zac seems to be quite a catch.'

Lisane felt Alain's hand tighten on hers as he pulled her in close. 'He's a nice man.'

What a tame description for someone of Zac's calibre! Yet what could she say? *He knocked me for six from the first moment I saw him?* That really would go down well, not to mention be hurtful.

'Very obviously wealthy.'

He sounded vaguely bitter, and, unless she was mistaken, jealous. Something for which she'd never given him cause during their friendship.

She looked at him carefully. 'I don't judge people by their wealth or lack of it.'

'Prominent barrister,' Alain continued. 'Attractive. And undoubtedly inventive between the sheets.'

Her eyes clouded a little. 'Stop right there,' she warned quietly. 'Or I'll walk off the floor.'

Alain lifted one eyebrow. 'At your sister's wedding? I doubt it.'

'Watch me.'

'My turn, I think?' Zac's indolent voice intervened, and there was something in the depths of his eyes that encouraged Alain to relinquish his hold.

Zac drew her in, and his gaze narrowed at the rapid-beating pulse at the base of her throat, the faint convulsive movement in her throat.

'Problems?'

'Nothing I can't handle.'

Except it wasn't the time or the place, and it saddened her Alain was using alcohol as a prop to quietly vent his feelings.

'He doesn't want to let go.'

She lifted her face to his. 'No.' It bothered her he hadn't managed to move on and make a life of his own. 'We grew up together. He wanted me to have the same feelings for him as Solene has for Jean-Claude.' She paused. 'Except to me,' she said quietly, 'he's always been the brother I never had.'

'His mother isn't helping the situation.' He made it a statement rather than a query. Chantelle had managed to sprinkle none too subtle hints into their conversation during the afternoon drive to and from her home.

Lisane managed a faint smile. 'You noticed, huh?'

The edges of his mouth twitched a little. 'You could say that.'

'Permissible evidence.'

Zac controlled the husky chuckle threatening to emerge from his throat as he splayed the hand resting at the back of her waist and drew her close against him. 'You might care to rephrase that.'

He saw the moment it hit her, and he delighted in the faint colour tinging her cheeks. 'It's become a little warm in here, don't you think?'

The light teasing quality in his voice was the polar opposite to the hard-hitting, merciless tone he employed in the court-room.

'I think you should behave,' she reproved with mock humour.

'Will you say that in a few hours' time?'

The mere thought momentarily trapped the air in her lungs and attacked the fragile tenure of her control.

'Anticipation is good for the soul,' Lisane offered primly, and heard his soft laughter.

'I shall take pleasure in proving you wrong.'

Imagining just how he'd achieve that caused her to almost miss a step.

'Perhaps we should circulate a little,' she managed, and wasn't sure whether to feel relieved or faintly peeved when he complied by leading her from the dance floor.

A prickling sensation niggled the back of her neck, almost as if someone was watching her every move. Alain? She didn't want to risk a skimming glance among the guests to check.

His disquiet...jealousy, she amended, was unexpected. Or was she simply being incredibly naive to hope he'd accept another man in her life?

Knowing she had a partner was one thing...being confronted with his physical presence was another.

Oh, give it up, she silently counselled. Hadn't she moved to another city in another state to start over so any relationship she formed wouldn't be in his face?

It was Solene and Jean-Claude's day. A beautiful wedding, followed by a lovely, relaxed, fun evening.

Any minute soon the bride and groom would bid their guests goodnight and leave for their hotel.

Almost on cue the DJ halted the music, and Henri, as master of ceremonies, took the microphone and announced Solene and Jean-Claude's departure.

It took a while, and Lisane was among the last to hug them both. 'Love you,' she bade as she attempted to hold on to her emotions.

'Right back at you.'

'See you tomorrow at the airport.'

Then they escaped into the waiting limousine.

Why did *happy* feel so sad? It didn't make sense!

Soon most of the guests had left, the gifts were loaded into a security van and Zac used his cellphone to summon a taxi.

Lisane bore Alain's narrowed gaze as she bade his parents 'goodnight', then she slipped into the taxi at Zac's side.

It had been an emotion-filled day, and one she'd relive many times as she examined photos and replayed the DVD.

Zac caught hold of her hand and lifted it to his lips. 'Tired?'

She looked at him, glimpsed the passion evident in those dark eyes, and smiled. 'If I was to say *yes*?'

'I'd promise to do all the work, then let you sleep.'

Desire, raw and primitive flooded her veins, and she aimed for a light-hearted response. 'Sounds like a plan.'

The night was dark with a pinprick of stars, and the only illumination was street-lights. Traffic was minimal, and the passage to Solene and Jean-Claude's Manly home was achieved in a short space of time.

Zac paid the driver while Lisane used her key to open the front door. The hall light sprang on, revealing some of the detritus of the day looking strangely out of place in Solene's normally immaculately kept home.

It wouldn't take long to set straight, and she began picking up, only to have Zac move to her side.

'Leave it until morning.'

His hands closed over her shoulders as he turned her round to face him, then he lowered his head and sought the sensitive curve at the edge of her neck, lingered there, then trailed up to settle at her temple.

Heat uncoiled from deep within and suffused her body, awakening each and every sensual pleasure point as she leant in against him.

Hands crept up and held his head fast as she slanted her

mouth against his, tasting his lips with the tip of her tongue as if she was beginning a tantalising sensual journey.

He possessed a beautifully shaped mouth, and she explored it at leisure, examining soft and hard tissue, the hard porcelain-like teeth, his tongue…delighting when it furled and began to slow-dance with her own.

It became more, so much more until the touching of mouths was no longer enough.

Lisane had lost awareness of where they were, and she told herself she didn't care. 'You're wearing too many clothes,' she managed, discovering somehow he'd shrugged out of his suit jacket and loosened his tie.

'So,' he said in a low and husky voice, 'take them off.'

Her fingers were deft in freeing his shirt buttons, and she undid the belt at his waist and loosened the top button of his trousers.

Zac toed off his shoes as they dealt with each other's zip fastening.

She loved the feel of him…the strength of his shoulders, the satiny skin covering taut musculature, and his narrow waist. Lean hips, tight buttocks, and the size and strength of his erection.

He found the slim satin edges of her thong and slid a finger beneath each seam at her hips and slipped them free, then he traced a path across her bikini line, tantalising in a way which had her responding in kind.

The only illumination came from the hall light, which cast a dimmed glow in the darkness of night.

Her fingers sought him, and she traced the hard length of his penis with a delicate touch, exploring the stretched foreskin with fascination, enjoying its smooth silkiness as it swelled beneath her feather-light finger-pad.

His body tensed, and she heard his husky groan as she brought him to the edge of control, then it was her turn to gasp as he sought her moist feminine heat and unerringly found the acutely sensitised clitoris.

Orgasm so strong it sprang in a rapidly spiralling coil through her body, and she gave an involuntary cry as he sent her to the brink, held her there, then fastened his mouth over hers as she fell.

The need to have him inside her was overpowering. In one fluid movement she straddled him, and felt his hands shift to cup her bottom.

'Patience, hmm?'

She heard his voice, and felt him move as he transferred them both down onto the bed.

Zac used his arms to support his weight as he began a slow tasting down the edge of her throat, savoured the sensitive hollow, then trailed to the soft fullness of her breast.

Lisane cried out as he explored the sensitive peak then took it into his mouth and suckled until she groaned with the intense pleasure before trailing to its twin and rendering a similar supplication.

The muscles in her belly quivered slightly as he moved lower, and she whimpered when he reached the highly sensitised heat and brought her to orgasm.

Just as she thought she could stand it no longer he positioned himself and entered her in one long thrust, filling her as she stretched to accommodate him.

It was almost more than she could bear, and she arched her body, then joined him in a sexual rhythm that took them both to the edge, held them there, then released them in a mutual sensual free-fall.

Wow. Lisane closed her eyes as the ecstasy diminished, not wanting it to leave the afterglow of sensational sex.

Lovemaking, she substituted. For her it had been more, so much more than just sex.

She felt Zac's lips brush her mouth, and she felt her own part beneath his.

It would be so easy to say *I love you.* And she almost did. Except she knew she'd die if she detected so much as a moment's hesitation in his response.

Zac eased himself from the bed, and moments later she heard the shower running, then he returned to gather her into his arms.

There was a dreamlike quality in standing beneath the shower-spray as he gently soaped her skin, and when he was done she took the soap tablet from his hand and returned the favour, loving the way his body tensed beneath her ministrations.

Afterwards, towelled dry, he carried her back to bed and curled her close in against him.

Lisane struggled through the veils of consciousness as the aroma of fresh coffee teased her nostrils. And there was the smell of food…was that bacon? Eggs? Toast?

'Come on, sleepyhead,' a familiar male voice teased huskily. 'Breakfast.'

She lifted her head from the pillow and looked at her wrist, only to realise she wasn't wearing a watch. 'What time is it?'

'Just a little after nine.'

Nine? That meant they only had an hour before they had to leave for the airport.

She took in Zac's tall frame attired in dress jeans and a chambray shirt and groaned out loud. 'You should have woken me.'

His smile almost melted her bones. 'I just did.'

'Before.'

'You were sleeping so peacefully it seemed a shame to disturb you.'

She sat up, realised she wasn't wearing a stitch and pulled the sheet high, only to hear his husky laughter.

'Come on, imp.' He reached for her robe and tossed it within reach. 'You can get dressed after you've eaten.'

It was only then they managed to catch up on each other's week…snatches of exchanged information as they ate, then cleared the dishes, and by the time she dressed, did something with her hair and added moisturiser and lip-gloss, it was time to leave.

'I wish you didn't have to go.'

Zac collected his overnight bag and hooked his suit-bag over one shoulder as she picked up the keys to Solene's car.

'Unfortunately I have to be in court first up tomorrow, and I have transcripts I need to read in order to put the finishing touches to my notes.'

Lisane knew the drill, appreciated its importance, and understood only too well. Except it didn't lessen the ache close to her heart at the thought of not seeing him for another two weeks.

Hell, two weeks seemed a lifetime!

Traffic was relatively easy on a Sunday morning, and they entered the airport terminal to find Chantelle, Henri and Alain waiting for them. Zac joined the appropriate queue and returned with his boarding pass just as Solene and Jean-Claude entered through the automatic doors.

They didn't have long together, only sufficient time for a few hugs and minimum conversation before the last call for Zac's flight was announced over the Tannoy.

Lisane felt her mouth tremble slightly as Zac lowered his head to hers, and nothing prepared her for the passion as his mouth possessed hers in a kiss that reached right into the heart and soul of her and branded her his own.

When he lifted his head his eyes gleamed dark, their expression enigmatic as they speared hers. 'I'll call you.'

He inclined his head towards Solene and Jean-Claude, Chantelle and Henri, Alain, then he turned and went through Security.

'Oh, my,' Solene murmured minutes later as she leaned in close to bid Lisane goodbye. 'That was something else. Take care, little sister.'

'Have a great holiday.'

'Bet your life on it.'

'That was the second call,' Jean-Claude warned, and after a quick hug they passed through into the security area.

'Would you like to come back to the house for lunch, Lisane?'

She glanced towards Alain and his parents, and tempered her refusal with a smile. 'I'd love to, but I have plans.'

'To catch up on some sleep?' Alain suggested.

Lisane ignored the faint edge in his voice and responded evenly, 'I'm sure we're all a bit tired from the wedding.' She met Chantelle's concerned gaze. 'Perhaps another time?'

'Of course, dear. We'll be in touch.'

She could have lingered a while. Probably should have, she reflected with some remorse as she drove out of the parking building and headed towards the city.

CHAPTER FIVE

LISANE spent the morning outdoors tending the garden beds along Solene's driveway, plucking out weeds and loosening the soil surrounding the hardy natives with their red and green foliage, the sturdy proteas and the clumps of busy-lizzies.

She examined the small expanse of lawn front and back of the house, decided it could do with some grooming, and retrieved the mower.

Sunshine, fresh air and achieving a neat garden was immensely satisfying, and the sun was edging high in the sky when she stowed the garden equipment in the garage.

A shower and change of clothes featured high on her list of priorities, and she had just locked the rear door when the front doorbell pealed.

Who? A salesman? Delivery guy?

Lisane checked the peep-hole, saw it was Jean-Claude's mother, and opened the door.

'Lisane.'

Chantelle greeted her with an affectionate smile. 'I was passing on my way to lunch with friends and thought I'd stop by and invite you to share dinner with us tonight.'

A kind woman who meant well, and whose invitation

she could hardly refuse. 'Love to. What time would you like me to be there?'

'Seven, sweetheart. I have some photos of the wedding. It'll be lovely to relax and catch up.'

Which reminded her to check her digital camera and run off some prints. 'I'll look forward to it.' She'd take a bottle of wine and collect flowers from the florist.

Which she took care of later in the afternoon.

Choosing what to wear to dinner didn't pose a problem, and she took pleasure in the pencil-slim black skirt and fitted blouse, dressed it with a tasteful drop pendant, added a few bracelets, put the finishing touches to her hair and make-up, then she slid her feet into stilettos and collected her bag.

Jean-Claude's parents resided in nearby Allambie Heights, and they both greeted her with a smattering of French and effusive warmth as they drew her into their home.

They were kind, well-meaning people of whom she was very fond…too well-meaning, she determined when Alain arrived minutes later.

She offered a polite smile as he crossed the room and brushed his lips to her cheek.

He was a pleasant man. Someone who would make a wonderful husband and father. So why hadn't she been able to love him as he deserved to be loved?

Was it so wrong to want the mesmeric hunger of primitive passion? To know a desire so strong it was almost shocking in its intensity?

And, having discovered both, to be aware that anything less could never be enough?

On the surface the ensuing few hours proved very

pleasant. A superb cook, Chantelle had excelled herself in presenting a gourmet meal of remembered favourite dishes from the days when Lisane and Solene had been frequent visitors.

On reflection, there were a number of 'remember when's sprinkled through the dinner conversation. Reminiscences that brought easy laughter, during which it was almost impossible not to experience a feeling of *déjà vu*.

'We miss you so much,' Chantelle offered with genuine sincerity. 'In another year or two, praise be, there will be a baby. It would be good for Solene to have you close.'

Lisane had a mental image of her sister pregnant with Jean-Claude's child, the babe itself, and felt the pull of familial loyalty. To share the day-to-day progress and rejoice in every small step would be incredible. Yet to do so would mean relocating to Sydney…and where would that leave her with Zac?

'Brisbane is only a one-hour forty-minute flight away.' Her warm smile was genuine. 'I'll visit often.'

'Ah, but if you were home, it would be better.'

'*Chérie,*' Henri chastised gently. 'Lisane has her own life, is this not so?' He didn't wait for an answer. 'Besides, who knows what the future will hold?'

'There is something you do not share with us?'

She suddenly became the focus of three pairs of eyes.

'Zac and I are very happy together,' she offered quietly.

It was almost possible to read Chantelle's mind: but my son has offered you *marriage.*

Did the official marriage certificate matter so much in the twenty-first century? If there were children, yes. But wasn't it possible to co-exist in a relationship with an agreement of mutual commitment?

For how long? A silent voice taunted.

Did she *want* permanence? To raise a family…grow old with him?

Her heart knew the answer. She just didn't want to go there right now.

'Then I am very pleased for you.'

But disappointed, Lisane added silently. 'Thank you.' She wanted to say more, but couldn't bring herself to voice the words.

'Coffee, *chérie*.' Henri's suggestion brought his wife to her feet.

'Of course.'

'Let me help you.' Lisane followed Chantelle into the kitchen, and took down cups and saucers while Chantelle fixed the coffee machine.

'It was a lovely meal, as always,' she complimented gently as they worked together with the ease of familiarity.

'You are most welcome. You know that.'

Yes, she did, and the knowledge brought a sense of sadness at having upset Chantelle's dearest wish to unite the younger Deveraux sister in marriage with her youngest son.

How could she explain to Alain's mother that, while she valued Alain's friendship, it wasn't possible to love to order? Nor was it fair for Chantelle to encourage him to hang in there on the off-chance Lisane might have a change of heart.

The coffee was done, and Chantelle loaded the tray. 'Let's go join the men, shall we?'

It was after ten when Lisane indicated a need to leave, and she thanked her hosts as Alain walked her out to the car.

She deactivated the alarm and turned towards him with a smile. 'Take care.'

'Always. And you.'

He lowered his head and brushed his lips to her cheek, then he found her mouth in a kiss with intent to seduce.

Don't, she silently begged. Don't do this. To me. To yourself.

She attempted to free herself, and he reluctantly let her go.

'Alain—'

'Old times' sake, Lisane?'

'Not fair.'

'Because I want to be with you?'

She should walk away…and almost did. 'We've already done this.' Her voice was quiet, steady. 'Nothing has changed.'

'So let's not do it again?'

'Please.' She crossed round to the driver's side, slid in behind the wheel and ignited the engine.

At the first set of lights she took the opportunity to switch on her cellphone, heard the familiar beep alert, checked messagebank and had time to read *Call me. Z.*

It didn't take long to reach Solene's Manly home, and she activated speed dial as soon as she stepped indoors.

Zac answered on the second ring, and the sound of his low-pitched drawl sent tiny curls of sensation spiralling deep within.

'Hi.' Her voice sounded husky to her own ears… choked, she amended as she summoned his image to mind without any effort at all.

'Missing me?'

Oh, yeah…in spades. 'A little,' she allowed, and heard his soft chuckle.

'Remind me to make up for it.'

Lisane settled down into a chair. 'Promises, promises. Where are you?'

'In bed.'

'Now, there's a provocative thought.' Extremely evocative, given he didn't wear a stitch beneath the sheets. All that smooth, tanned skin stretched sleek over powerful musculature.

She could almost sense his male scent, the clean smell of soap lingering on his skin from a recent shower…and felt her bones begin to melt.

'How was your day?'

Lisane relayed it in brief detail, adding, 'I spent the evening with Jean-Claude's parents.' Honesty compelled her to include, 'Alain was there.'

'Naturally.'

It was easy to slip into teasing mode. 'That bothers you?'

'Should it?'

'And here I was, afraid you might be jealous.'

'He has my sympathy.'

The evocative factor moved up a notch. She wanted so badly to be with him, it was almost a physical pain.

'No response, Lisane?'

'You want flippant…or deeply serious?'

'The latter might lead to something too hard to handle.'

A light laugh escaped her lips. 'Titillating phone sex, Zac?'

'A very inadequate substitute.' There was humour in his voice.

Wasn't that the truth! 'How's the case going?'

'Opposing counsel has built a strong defence.'

He would be exploring every angle, attempting to gain any edge. 'Too strong?'

'Difficult,' Zac conceded.

'You predict he'll walk?'

'Not if I can help it.'

His expertise in the criminal-law field was well-known, and lauded by his contemporaries in the justice system. A reputation that had gained him a few enemies over time.

'Don't work too hard.' The light caution held genuine concern, and she could sense his answering smile.

'Sweet dreams. I'll call in a few days.'

Lisane heard the faint click as he cut the connection, and she did likewise, taking time to reflect on their conversation as she checked Security before entering her room.

Sleep came easily…too easily, for Lisane woke as dawn was breaking, caught the reality, and closed her eyes in the hope of slipping back into a subconscious lulled by erotic imaginings too highly sensual to want to let go.

Except it wasn't going to happen, and, after a few minutes spent reviewing her plans for the day, she swept the bedcovers aside and stood to her feet.

Whoa. Not such a good idea. Her head wasn't sure if it belonged on her body, and there was a war going on in her stomach.

Something she'd eaten last night?

The escargot? Chicken fricassée? The delicious torte?

Whatever, it wasn't going to stay down.

OK, she reasoned several minutes later after brushing her teeth and rinsing her mouth out. Somewhere, somehow, she'd developed a stomach bug. Twenty-four hours of bland food, plenty of water, and she'd be fine.

Dry toast and an apple proved to be a good strategy, and she busied herself sorting the various boxes of wedding gifts delivered soon after nine. Something which brought vivid memories of the wedding itself.

Then it was time to change and drive into the city to meet lifelong friends Alyse, Karen and Gigi for lunch.

Smart casual wear would suffice, and she stepped into dress jeans, added a fashionable cotton top, then slid her feet into stilettos.

A restaurant at Darling Harbour overlooking the water was their venue of choice, and she was first to arrive.

Sunlight kissed the smooth water's surface, giving it a dappled effect with shadows cast from nearby high-rise hotel, office and apartment buildings.

A favoured area of many, Darling Harbour featured several restaurants and a large shopping complex, with easy access from the inner city.

Admired and frequented by day and by night, it drew patrons and tourists alike.

Lisane followed the *maître d'* to their reserved table, accepted a glass of iced water, and withheld perusing the menu until she was joined by her friends.

'Hey,' a warm feminine voice greeted minutes later, and was doubly echoed as Alyse, Karen and Gigi moved in close to exchange fond hugs in greeting. 'We have an hour…well, forty-five minutes.' They each took a seat and checked out the menu. 'Let's order, shall we?'

Lisane chose something light, and it was wonderful to relax in the company of good friends, to gossip and catch up, to laugh a little.

'OK, *give*,' Alyse begged as the waiter delivered their meal. 'I want to know more about that gorgeous spunky partner of yours.' She offered an impish grin. 'And does he have a brother? A cousin? *Any* male relative who looks and acts like such fabulous eye-candy?'

'An uncle, if you fancy the over-forty male. And there's a cousin or two.'

'Yes, please. Name, phone number.'

Lisane offered a mischievous smile. 'Only a slight problem there.'

Alyse leant forward. 'No problem is insurmountable.'

'The cousins reside in America.' There was a collective audible groan. 'And the uncle lives in London.'

'Oh, well, there goes the master plan.' Alyse's eyes twinkled with devilish fun. 'Moving right along...when can we expect to see a ring on your finger?'

Here we go. The third degree, as only long-time friends can conduct an interrogation! 'You'll be among the first to know.'

'Tight as a clam,' Karen offered. 'Well, that's OK. Just make sure you issue an invite for the big day.'

Why confide the possibility that it may not happen?

Lisane reached into her bag and extracted a slender packet. 'I've brought some photos.'

The best of the best, which Alyse, Karen and Gigi exclaimed over with enthusiasm, from Solene's dress, the flowers, cake, to the groom's brother.

'Did I detect a little one-upmanship going on with Alain?'

A slight understatement, and thankfully out of sight and hearing of most of the guests.

'Did you know he talks about you all the time?' Gigi offered quietly.

'The man needs to move on.' Karen cast Gigi a faint frown.

Lisane picked up on the subtext. Gigi was perfect for Alain. 'Go for it.' Her enthusiasm was genuine, and glimpsed

Gigi's slightly anguished expression. 'I mean it. If you want my blessing…it's yours.'

'There's no chance—'

'None at all,' she said gently.

Alyse checked her watch. 'Five minutes, girls.' She turned to Lisane. 'We're doing dinner and the movies tomorrow evening. Join us.'

'Done. Tell me what time and where, and I'll be there.'

'I'll SMS you.'

They had the waiter bring the bill, settled it, then walked out onto the quay, said 'goodbye', and Lisane elected to browse the shops awhile before heading for the northern suburbs.

Dinner comprised a salad and fresh fruit, after which she slotted in a DVD, watched it, then collected the new suspense novel she'd bought and retired to bed.

The sun was casting bright strips of light through the wooden shutters masking the bedroom window when Lisane came awake and aware she'd slept in.

Eight-thirty? For heaven's sake, why so late?

There were a number of things she wanted to do with the day…so rise and shine, dress, have breakfast and make a start.

She slid out of bed, stood to her feet…and felt her stomach execute a few vicious rolls, necessitating a speedy path to the bathroom.

Again? Maybe the stomach bug was alive and well and determined to stay on for another day.

OK, so she'd deal with it, try for another bland breakfast, and hope for the best.

A suspicious niggle had her doing the maths…and she

came to the conclusion there was no chance. Besides, she was on the Pill…admittedly low dosage, but it hadn't failed her before. So why should she imagine it might do so now?

She made a deal with herself. If the symptoms persisted, she'd purchase a pregnancy-testing kit. It would be easy enough to dispense with if it wasn't needed.

But what if…? No, she wouldn't go there.

Busy. She'd plan the next few days allowing the minimum time in which to think.

It worked mostly because she bought fabric and used Solene's sewing machine to make two casual cotton tops and a tailored skirt suitable for the office.

The cinemaplex Alyse nominated formed part of a large shopping complex with several restaurants and cafe's available for in-house and outdoor dining, and they chose a pavement café for a light meal before buying tickets for the highly awarded film which had scooped the Oscar pool.

There could be no doubt why the film was such a success, for the acting, direction and cinematography were excellent.

Lisane declined extending the evening by sharing coffee, and took Karen's gentle teasing,

'We know. You want to rush off and call Zac. Go for it, girl. If I had a hunk like him waiting for me on the other end of a phone, I wouldn't hang around either.'

Except when she reached the house and checked, there were no messages on her cellphone.

No, no, *no*. Not again, Lisane groaned as she hit the ground running. Two more mornings of this didn't bode well.

There was nothing else for it but to retrieve the pregnancy-testing kit and do the test, and her fingers shook as she extracted the relevant equipment.

The instructions were clear, and she took a deep breath, uttered a silent prayer…and waited for the result.

It was crazy not to want to look, and she did a silent count to ten before she checked…then she leant back against the tiled wall and slid down to sit on the floor.

Pregnant. She was *pregnant*.

Dear lord in heaven…what was she going to do?

OK, so the test didn't offer a one hundred per cent certainty. What if it was wrong?

There was only one way to find out for sure, and she checked the time, the local doctor's surgery hours, saw she had an hour before she could dial the listed number…and showered, dressed, then had breakfast.

Ten more minutes.

The longest minutes in the known universe before she keyed in the number, pleaded urgency and managed to secure a mid-morning appointment.

It was impossible to stay still, and after half an hour of pacing the floor she tied back her hair, added lip-gloss, collected her bag and drove to the medical centre.

With half an hour to spare, she bought the day's newspaper, crossed to a nearby café, ordered a cup of tea and filled in time leafing through the pages.

Overseas section, local news, social column…

A newsprint photo looked incredibly familiar, and she took a closer look.

Allegra Fabrisi? Featured in a Sydney newspaper?

Lisane skimmed the newsprint, and almost reeled with shock.

Allegra Fabrisi, barrister and daughter of eminent Brisbane judge Leo Fabrisi, is expected to announce her engagement soon to a prominent Brisbane barrister and member of the wealthy Winstone family.

Did hearts stop?

For a moment she felt as if she couldn't breathe.

Dear God. *Zac?*

Had to be. Unless…

No, not even Allegra would resort to initiating a false statement…surely?

Get a grip. There was only one way to handle this. She needed to speak with Zac.

So do it, why don't you? a tiny voice prompted.

Except he'd be in court and beyond contact except in a dire emergency. And somehow an SMS wouldn't cut it.

Instead she put a call through to his chambers and left a message for him to contact her that evening.

Lisane wasn't conscious of how long she sat there, or of the people walking by, the sound of traffic, or the occasional blast of a car horn.

All these months had she just been a convenient bed partner? A fill-in for the woman destined to be Zac's wife? The many nights of lovemaking, the sharing of primitive passion…was it all faked on his part?

Yet none of it seemed to equate with the man she thought she knew so well.

Lisane closed her eyes, then opened them again.

Time. What was the time?

A quick glance at her watch revealed she was due in the

doctor's surgery *now*, and she caught up her bag and crossed into the medical centre.

Half an hour later she retraced her steps and ordered more tea. Hot and sweet in the hope it would soothe her shattered nerves.

Seven weeks pregnant.

It didn't seem possible. Except the doctor had explained precisely how the low-dose Pill was rendered ineffective for the month if there was more than a thirty-six-hour gap between dosage. Narrowing it down, with some pertinent prompting, she was able to pinpoint it to a gastric attack during late August.

'I take it this isn't a planned pregnancy?'

The doctor's words reiterated themselves several times inside her head, and she didn't know whether to laugh or cry.

She was pregnant to a man who was about to become engaged to another woman.

Oh, *hell*. What was she going to do?

Worse, who could she confide in?

No one, except her sister, and Solene wasn't due back in Sydney until Saturday.

The rest of the day passed in a blur as she examined her options, and, although termination was one of them, she knew deep down she'd never be able to bring herself to do it.

Single-motherhood.

Something which would mean relocation from Brisbane.

A slightly hysterical laugh rose in her throat at the thought of flaunting her pregnant belly in the court corridors frequented by both Zac and Allegra.

Not funny!

There was, of course, the slim chance Allegra had deliberately orchestrated the reference to the Winstone family, and it wasn't Zac.

Sure, and pigs might fly.

Lisane forced herself to eat an evening meal and viewed television vacantly as she waited for Zac to call.

When the phone rang at seven she snatched it up and voiced a faintly breathless 'hello'…only to discover it was Alain, not Zac, and she curbed her impatience with effort.

'I want to apologise for last night. I was way out of line.'

Please. I don't need this right now. 'Alain—'

'I thought maybe we could go somewhere,' he intercepted quickly. 'Share a coffee, take in a movie. As friends,' he added. 'Nothing more.'

'Thanks, but—'

'No thanks?'

'I think I'm coming down with something.' Something due to hang around for another seven months…before emerging to become a lifetime commitment!

'Take care.'

'I'll be fine.' Sure, she acceded with a degree of cynicism. She was anything but *fine*.

She couldn't settle, and after channel-surfing she switched off the television and picked up a novel…only to discard it after fruitlessly reading pages without absorbing a word.

Zac…where the hell are you?

OK, she'd wait half an hour, then she'd call *him*.

Except when she did, the call went straight to his messagebank.

Lisane woke several times during the night, checked the time, then her cellphone, and finally slid into a deep sleep from which the insistent burr of the cellphone early next morning had her fumbling for the phone.

'Did I wake you?' Zac's husky voice held amusement as she struggled into a sitting position.

'I slept in.'

'You sound surprised. Late night?'

'In a manner of speaking. You?'

'Dinner with family and friends.'

Lisane closed her eyes, then opened them again. 'Of whom Allegra was one?'

'Yes.'

So it was true. 'Should I congratulate you?'

There was a second's silence. 'Congratulations are a little premature. The news isn't official.'

Almost on cue her stomach roiled, and she barely had time to offer, 'I'll call you back,' before dashing from the bed into the bathroom.

Dear heaven. *This* was morning sickness?

Saturday arrived. With unhurried movements Lisane cleaned up as usual, then dressed in jeans and a top before entering the kitchen to prepare breakfast.

Afterwards she cleaned the house, then shopped to re-stock Solene's pantry in preparation for her sister's return.

Activities which occupied her hands, but did little or nothing to detract from the host of chaotic thoughts and images swirling inside her brain.

The first and foremost being…*how could he?*

Several times she castigated herself for being a fool. Hadn't all the signs been evident?

Yet she'd gone with her heart instead of listening to her head. *Fool.*

Lisane left for the airport mid-afternoon, thankful that Solene and Jean-Claude's flight was on time, and their enthusiastic, laughter-filled reunion did much to lighten Lisane's mood.

Everything was wonderful…Hayman Island, the accommodation, food, swimming.

'We're going back for our first wedding anniversary,' Solene determined as she leant back against her husband's chest.

Lisane kept her smile in place and fought back the threat of tears. Damn, this was hard! She was on an emotional see-saw that swung every which way but loose.

By evening she felt as if her face would crack from the strain of keeping a smile in place, and she nursed a headache that seemed to worsen by the hour until she pleaded the need for an early night.

Sunday brought little improvement, with a busy morning preparing food for a celebratory lunch Solene and Jean-Claude were hosting for family and friends arranged to view the opening of their wedding gifts.

It was a casual meal, buffet-style, held outdoors in the back garden, and fun and laughter, mixing and mingling, made for an enjoyable hour before the main gift-opening event.

Lisane was appointed to write each gift item against the prepared list of invited guests, and it was almost six when the last person departed.

'Let's vote to skip dinner in favour of eating leftovers,' Solene suggested, and received a unanimous *yes*.

Within minutes they'd each filled a plate and sat eating picnic-style at the kitchen table.

'If you don't mind,' Jean-Claude began as he finished his meal, 'I'll go transfer our holiday photos onto the laptop and print them.' He leant forward and brushed his lips to Solene's cheek. 'You girls can exchange girl-talk.'

CHAPTER SIX

'OK, WHAT'S up?'

Oh, heavens. Sisterly inquisition, with no leading preliminary! 'What makes you think something's wrong?' Calm, rational words that merely brought forth a narrowed look.

'Because you're pale, dark-eyed…and I can read you like a book.'

So much for bright conversation, light laughter and affectionate warmth. 'I caught a stomach bug.' Could a tiny foetus loosely fit that description? She barely resisted the impulse to place a protective hand over her stomach and murmur an apology.

'How long have you had it?'

Oh, around two months. Except her knowledge extended to only a few days. 'Since mid-week.' Truth by omission. The question was whether Solene would accept it without further enquiry.

Fat chance.

'Everything OK between you and Zac?'

Just brilliant. 'I understand he's about to become engaged.'

Her sister's eyes sharpened. 'And you know this...
because?'

'There was an announcement in the daily newspaper.'

Solene's expression resembled a mother hen fussing
over a lonely chick. 'Let me see the news-clipping.'

Lisane retrieved it and placed the slip of newsprint in
Solene's outstretched hand, watching as she skimmed the
brief announcement before carefully putting it to one side.

'You've checked the Brisbane-based papers?'

Every page, each article. 'Yes.'

'*And?*'

'The announcement is identical.'

'Unusual, don't you think? Given the Winstone and
Fabrisi families are in the top echelon of Brisbane society?
One would expect to see a photo of the happy couple, some
journalistic detail and an indication of when the wedding
will take place.'

Hadn't she puzzled over the same thing? Examining
every angle until it had almost driven her mad?

'You haven't considered Allegra could be responsible?'

Oh, yes. Every minute of every day...let's not even
count the nights! She wasn't conscious of biting the edge
of her lip until there was the faint sting of pain.

Solene offered a thoughtful look tinged with an edge
of cynicism. 'What does she have to lose? If confronted
with the announcement all she has to do is provide a
suitable statement citing misinterpretation of the spoken
word and blame the journalist.'

That much made perfect sense. Allegra possessed the
ability to twist the English language every which way...in
the court-room, and out of it.

'What was Zac's reaction?'

Lisane endeavoured to hide the pain encompassing her body. Dammit, why did it have to hurt so much? 'I need to call him.'

'And you *haven't*?'

Lisane's silence succeeded in edging her sister's speculation up a notch.

'OK. *Give*. The whole story. And don't leave anything out.'

Two sisters who knew each other a little too well for either one to be fooled by the other.

What was the point in prevaricating? 'I'm pregnant.' There, she'd said it.

Solene dispensed with the niceties, and got straight to the point. 'How long have you known?'

It seemed like a lifetime. 'Five days.'

'You've had the pregnancy confirmed?'

The doctor's visit was indelibly imprinted on her brain, and his diagnosis had haunted her ever since. 'Yes.'

'You have to tell Zac,' her sister said quietly.

Lisane rolled her eyes, unsure whether to laugh or cry. 'You think?'

Solene frowned. 'Don't be facetious.'

Delaying it wouldn't gain a thing. Hadn't she lain awake at night composing numerous words to convey the news? Only to discard each and every one of them.

She could just imagine how that would go, especially if she caught him at an inconvenient time. And when wouldn't it be an inconvenient time? During the day was impossible…he'd be caught up in chambers, in court, consulting with a client and his solicitor. Important stuff that shouldn't be interrupted, except in an emergency situation.

Did enlightening he was going to become a parent fall under *emergency*? Somehow she didn't think so.

Evenings? He was in the middle of an important case. He'd be examining court transcripts, searching for an edge, preparing notes…

'You're not considering a termination?'

Lisane lifted a hand, then let it fall helplessly to her side. 'You think I haven't agonised over this?' she demanded wretchedly. A child was a precious gift. One she could never willingly destroy.

Yet the solution brought up the question of parental rights, reaching an agreement to share the responsibility of raising a child. It was more than financial obligation…the physicality of sharing in the child's upbringing raised numerous questions.

The most glaring one being how she could bear to agree to her child being nurtured by Allegra as Zac's wife in a custody agreement.

If in fact the proposed marriage was a reality.

She closed her eyes against the painful image, and aimed for a semblance of calm as for the hundredth time she reflected on the passion evident in Zac's kiss minutes before he boarded the flight to Brisbane.

Could he have faked it?

Surely not. Unless he'd faked everything about their relationship, and she'd been just a convenient body willing to share herself with him…for as long as it lasted.

Was that all she was to him?

Had Allegra been right in intimating approval of him 'having a little sexual freedom' before settling into marriage…with her?

'Hey, stop with the agony, already.' Solene reached

forward and enveloped her in a sisterly hug. 'It's Sunday evening. SMS his cellphone and ask him to call.'

Why did it feel such a leap of faith? Wanting to hear his voice, yet dreading what he might have to say.

'Don't think,' her sister bade gently. 'Just do it.'

Hesitation wouldn't solve a thing, and with a sense of fatalism she caught up her cellphone and keyed in a brief message, checked and then sent it.

'I'll make a cup of tea.'

The panacea for all ills in a time of need, Lisane reflected silently, and felt her stomach execute a slow twist as the minutes ticked by...and her cellphone didn't ring.

'Maybe he doesn't have it with him.'

Sure, as if that was likely. He *always* carried it, and had messagebank activated if he wasn't able to take a call.

Lisane accepted the tea, refused anything to eat and tried to ignore the nerves knotting inside her stomach.

Logic rationalised Zac would eventually check his cellphone, and when he did he might consider it was too late to call.

Oh, *hell*...why did life have to suddenly become so complicated?

'Want to watch a movie on DVD?'

She caught her sister's caring expression, the underlying commiseration, and knew if she didn't *do* something she'd end up in tears. Hormones swinging every which way but loose!

'I'll probably fall asleep. Around nine my body shuts down like a light.' Too true, and right on cue the tiredness began to envelop her like a shroud. 'If you don't mind, I'll catch an early night.' She stood to her feet and trailed gentle fingers down Solene's cheek. 'Thanks for being there.'

'Always.'

The guest bedroom was only a few steps down the hallway, and Lisane quietly closed the door behind her, then began discarding her clothes.

Minutes later she sat propped up in bed and reached for a book filled with mischief, mayhem and gripping suspense in the hope she'd become immersed in the characters, the plot.

It worked to a degree, and each time her mind wandered she dragged it back to the printed word. Until the page became a blur and the book slid from her fingers.

Turn the light off and go to *sleep*, for heaven's sake, an inner voice dictated, and she reached for the bedside lamp in silent obedience…only to hear the definitive burr of her cellphone.

For a few heart-stopping seconds she couldn't move, then fear the call would end before she picked up galvanised her into action.

Recognition of the caller ID increased her nervous tension, and her 'hello' sounded breathless even to her own ears.

'Lisane.' His deep drawl tugged her heartstrings, and there was little she could do about the pain skittering through her body. 'I've just accessed my phone.'

It took resolve to keep her voice light. 'You've been working?'

'A dinner break which lasted longer than anticipated.'

She just stopped herself from asking *with whom*? 'How's the case going?'

'Reasonably well.'

'That's good.'

Coward. Cut the niceties…and tell him!

The words spilt out. 'I wanted to offer my congratulations.' She waited a beat, then offered quietly. 'Perhaps you should check last Tuesday's paper. Page five, right-hand column.' Without cohesive thought she cut the connection.

There, she'd done it.

Only to have her cellphone give its distinctive burr mere seconds later. Except she didn't pick up.

Over the next several minutes it rang on two more occasions. With resolve she activated messagebank and switched off the cellphone.

It was late. Too late to be considered a reasonable hour for anyone to place a call to the house-line. And dammit, she refused to check for any messages to her cellphone.

Morning would be soon enough.

Lisane fell asleep soon after her head touched the pillow. Something which came as a surprise when she woke next morning, for somehow she'd expected to lay awake agonising over hanging up on Zac's call...worse, choosing not to pick up when he rang back.

It was still early. The house was quiet, although she could hear birds twittering in the trees outside her window. Somewhere a door slammed, a car engine fired, and in the distance a dog barked. Soon to be joined by other dogs in tandem.

She resisted the temptation to turn on her cellphone and check for messages, discarding it on a 'need-to-know' basis. Later, when she was dressed and had settled her stomach with tea and toast...maybe then.

Sunshine filtered through the curtains, fingering the room with warmth, and minutes later she tossed back the bedcovers and cautiously swung her feet to the floor.

So far, so good. Maybe if she moved slowly the desire to heave would be averted.

Sure! Three steps and she had to break into a run to reach the *en suite*. Six-to-eight more weeks of this, and she'd be a wreck. The thought she might be in the minority of women who suffered thus through the entire pregnancy brought her out in a sweat!

A shower helped, and she put on jeans and a top, pulled her hair into a loose knot at her nape, then she emerged from her room and made her way to the kitchen.

The aroma of freshly brewed coffee teased her taste-buds and accelerated a craving for her usual morning caffeine fix. Tea just didn't seem a satisfactory substitute!

Solene was stacking toast onto a plate with one hand while the other dipped a teabag into a cup of hot water. Bacon sizzled in the pan, almost perfectly crisp and ready to serve.

'Hi.' Lisane breathed in with appreciation. 'Smells great.'

Her sister turned and shook her head in dismay. 'You're not supposed to be here.'

Lisane arched an eyebrow. 'Where else should I be?'

'In your room. I was going to bring you breakfast in bed.' Solene gestured towards the table. 'Go sit down.'

Solene in older-sister mode was quite something!

She effected a mock salute. 'Yes, ma'am.' And did what she was told.

'Jean-Claude?'

'He left early to meet Alain. They're taking the boat out for the day.'

A plate of bacon and eggs was placed in front of Lisane. 'Eat!'

'Thanks,' she said gratefully. 'My turn to cook tomorrow.'

Solene pulled out a chair opposite, took a sip of ruinously black coffee, then nursed the cup in both hands.

Lisane picked up cutlery and cut into a strip of bacon, added some egg and forked the morsel into her mouth. Ambrosia.

'Are you OK?'

Now, there was a telling question! She cut straight to the chase. 'Zac rang. We spoke. I hung up on him.'

Her sister's eyes sharpened a little. 'I'm interested in the *we spoke* part between "Zac rang" and "I hung up on him".'

'Basically the conversation was limited.' On reflection, she hadn't really given him a chance. But then the jury was out as to whether he deserved it or not. 'I suggested he check the newspaper…I offered the date, page number and appropriate column.'

She cut a small square of toast and added bacon and egg, ate it and followed it with a mouthful of tea.

'One assumes he rang back?'

'A few times.'

'And?'

'I let messagebank take any further calls, then turned off the cellphone.'

Pensive doubt clouded her sister's gaze. 'You've checked for messages.'

A statement, not a query. Lisane rolled her eyes. 'Not yet.'

'Don't you think you should?'

'I will. Eventually.'

Solene leant forward slightly. 'Do you really think that's the best way to handle the situation?'

The clear ringing tone of the land-line provided an intrusion, and Lisane carefully replaced her cutlery. 'If that's Zac, tell him I'm in the shower.'

Coward. She needed to know…yet she didn't want to hear what he had to say. Which was a conundrum, and at variance with common sense.

'Please.'

Solene shook her head in slight exasperation, crossed to pick up the receiver, and relayed the customary greeting while Lisane watched and listened to her sister handle Zac's queries as if nothing were amiss.

Damn, but she was good!

The conversation didn't go over-long, and Lisane waited until her sister cut the connection.

'Thanks.' The word was heartfelt, and earned her a wry smile.

'He wants you to return his call.'

Butterflies began beating their wings inside her stomach…or at least, that was what it felt like!

'Go check your cellphone for messages.'

She could do that. Should have done it as soon as she woke. Except morning sickness had intervened, and afterwards the need for food seemed more important.

Oh, for heaven's sake! Whatever SMS message Zac had sent her was *there*. To delay checking what he'd said was ridiculous!

Minutes later she switched between three printed texts on the small screen.

Pick up.

Call me.

We need to talk.

Lisane silently handed the slim phone to her sister, who skimmed the text and handed it back.

'You can't delay calling him.'

She met Solene's gaze…eyes as blue as her own, and filled with concern.

'But first,' she ventured quietly, and tried to still the way her stomach began to churn, 'I need a plan.'

'Which you've already given some thought?'

How could she not have done? Her mind had been tortured with various scenarios since confirmation of her pregnancy.

The one constant was her decision to keep the child.

'The only solution,' Lisane began with quiet resolve, 'is to end the relationship, give in my notice and relocate.'

'You think Zac will accept that?'

She gave a slight shrug. 'We're just…friends and lovers. No commitment given or expected.'

Except it was more than that. Much more. For her.

No man, other than Zac, had the power to make her *feel* so much. He was her light, the very air she breathed. Everything.

Love?

Did love play untold havoc with your emotions? Or was it just pregnancy hormones?

How was she to know for sure?

Solene leaned forward and caught both Lisane's hands in her own. 'It's not like you to run away from anything.'

'No?' She barely kept the scepticism from her voice. 'What about when the heat became unbearable with Alain?'

'You left…after you had the courage to tell him how you felt.'

She was unable to prevent a faint wryness in her tone. 'Alain has a different perspective.'

'He loved you. Still does.'

It made her heart ache she couldn't love him the same way.

'I can't see Zac not wanting to share in his child's life.'

She didn't know his stance on children. The subject hadn't arisen. 'It's better I relocate.'

She could lease out her cottage … her mind raced ahead with alternatives, weighing up options.

'Leaving Brisbane is *Plan B*,' Solene assured.

'And what do you perceive as *Plan A*?' Even as she launched the question, she already knew the answer. 'Something permanent?' For a moment she felt as if she couldn't breathe. *'Marriage?* Because it would be the *right* thing to do?' She shook her head in silent negation. 'Don't even go there.'

'OK, let's return to *Plan B*,' Solene ventured with ease. 'If you decide to relocate, why not Sydney, where I can be on hand with some back-up? You could stay here until you get settled in a new job and find a place of your own.'

She felt as if she was going to cry. 'You're a sweetheart, and I appreciate the offer.'

'Why do I get the feeling there's a *but* in there?'

Did ambivalence fall into the pregnancy hormonal basket? Along with contrariness and indecision?

Her sister's concern was palpable. 'Promise me you won't make any decisions until you've talked to Zac.'

As if she wanted to do that any time soon! Yet putting it off wasn't going to help.

'Let's go shopping. Lunch is on me.' People, shops, coffee—*tea*, she silently corrected—and bright conversation. Maybe they'd even fit in a facial and manicure… anything as a distraction from her dilemma.

'OK. Why not aim for the best?' Solene swung easily into the mood with a teasing smile. 'Double Bay?'

'It's a date.' Lisane collected her cellphone and sought the privacy of her bedroom in which to make the call.

Zac answered on the third ring, and the sound of his voice succeeded in twisting her stomach into an impossible knot.

'You have some explaining to do.'

Pent-up anger held tightly in check was evident, and she retaliated in kind.

'So do you.'

'Allegra.'

'Uh-huh.' Chameleon, witch and superb actress.

'A journalistic misunderstanding.'

Sure, and piglets fly! Strike one for the very clever attorney.

She didn't know whether to laugh or cry…because it didn't change a thing.

'Why don't you catch the next flight home?'

The huskiness in his voice did strange things to her equilibrium, and she clenched her fingers against the urge to say *yes*.

She could almost feel the warmth of his arms, the touch of his mouth against her own. The sweet sorcery that was theirs alone. Her body craved his with a need that shook her slim frame.

He'd captured her heart, but she had to think with her head.

Oh, dear lord, why did it have to be so difficult? 'I've decided to base myself in Sydney.'

There was a moment's silence. 'Perhaps you'd care to run that by me again.' His voice was too quiet, and so controlled it sent shivers down her spine.

'It's a decision I'm entitled to make,' she reminded with polite civility. Difficult, when she was weeping inside, and there was a need to sit down before she slid ignominiously to the floor.

'Accept it's over, Zac.' She cut the connection before he could offer a further word, and the finality of her action was almost more than she could bear.

For what seemed an age she sat frozen in silence. Waiting for *what*…Zac to call back? Oh, *please*, give it a break. It's done. Over.

So get on with it, why don't you?

Splash your face with cold water, change your clothes, apply make-up, then go try to enjoy the day.

Actions she completed on autopilot, and she practised a bright smile as she joined Solene, who took one look and wisely refrained from offering a word.

'Let's hit the shops.'

They did, checking out the window displays in exclusive Double Bay, entering selective boutiques to examine and try on a variety of clothing, beautiful Manolo Blahnik shoes too ruinously expensive for their individual budgets…but fun to let their imaginations soar with boundless possibilities should they ever have the resources to indulge in such luxuries.

'Lunch,' Lisane determined as they exited from yet another boutique. 'I'm starving.'

That was another thing she was beginning to discover about the effects of early pregnancy…food. The taste, texture, and particularly its aroma appeared to have heightened and changed.

The restaurant Lisane chose was upmarket, mostly filled with the 'in' crowd. Society matrons meeting to nibble at small portions of fine food and exchange gossip, partners sharing a business lunch, and the occasional roue holding court with the woman *de jour*.

The temptation to check her cellphone for messages was difficult to resist.

'Do you want to talk about it?'

The waiter had poured iced water into their glasses, taken their order, and there was that pleasant anticipatory lull of a shared meal in good company.

Lisane didn't pretend to misunderstand. 'Not particularly.' She took a sip of water, then replaced the glass onto the table.

Reality began to hit, with all its ramifications, despite her belief in having made the only decision she considered feasible.

Handing in her resignation was one thing…citing a family crisis would ensure she worked out minimum notice. Which meant she'd be in the court stream and likely to see Zac, even in passing.

Would they acknowledge each other?

Oh, come on … get a grip! *You* ended the relationship, remember?

It was the sensible thing to do.

Wasn't it?

So why did it have to hurt so much?

The waiter delivered their meal, smoked salmon curled over a potato-salad stack and topped with a generous rocket salad. Eaten at leisure and washed down with iced water, it made for a pleasant meal.

Look at the big picture, a silent voice intruded. Sydney, having Solene's support, a new job…and a beautiful child. A part of Zac that would be unquestionably hers for the rest of her life.

And his.

Something she was morally bound to tell him, and she should have…except it hadn't seemed appropriate to convey news of his impending fatherhood over the phone.

Oh, why not tell it like it is? At the last minute, she'd chickened out.

How could she say… *By the way, I'm pregnant. What are we going to do about it?*

Lisane closed her eyes briefly, then opened them again.

This time last week her life had been good. Now it was topsy-turvy with a number of complications.

'Would you prefer coffee or tea?'

They lingered a while, taking the opportunity to catch up on the more prosaic aspects of their lives before continuing a leisurely browse among several boutiques lining both sides of the street.

It was after five when Solene pulled into the driveway behind Jean-Claude's four-wheel drive.

Fresh salad and a baguette rested on the kitchen servery, and Jean-Claude and Alain could be seen out back readying the barbecue.

'Good to see you making yourselves useful,' Solene teased as she lifted her face for her husband's lingering kiss.

Lisane dampened down the tiny spiral of emotion, and moved to Alain's side. 'I gather it was a satisfactory fishing jaunt.'

'Very. We managed to cover a lot.'

'Brotherly companionship, huh?'

His steady gaze held a quality she didn't want to examine. 'You could say that.'

Jean-Claude wouldn't have confided her predicament in Alain, surely?

'I'll go change,' she managed quietly. 'A dress and heels aren't exactly back-yard barbecue wear.'

Jeans and a top, she decided as she reached her room,

and she quickly effected the change before slipping her feet into sandals.

When she emerged it was to find Alain waiting for her in the kitchen, and his expression held a degree of purpose that made her heart sink a little.

'Alain, please.'

'Just...hear me out.'

Please don't do this, she begged silently.

'I can offer you marriage. Be a father to your child in every way, including adoption.'

This was the man with whom she'd shared her childhood, friend, confidant...someone she could trust with her life.

'I appreciate it,' she said gently. 'Really. But you deserve someone who loves you.'

He took hold of her hands. 'Whatever you offered me would be enough.'

No, it wouldn't. Not when my heart and soul belong to someone else. My child. How could I lie with you at night and pretend you were another? You'd know. You couldn't help but know.

Words she couldn't say. Wouldn't, because it would hurt him more than he needed to be hurt.

'I care for you.' She removed her hands from his grasp. 'Too much to take advantage.'

He opened his mouth to speak, and she pressed a finger to his lips. 'So, let me thank you from the bottom of my heart. And promise, should I ever need your help I'll ask you for it.' She laid the palm of her hand over his cheek. 'Let's go outside and join the others, shall we?'

Alain didn't move. 'You won't,' he managed in a voice that mirrored his dejection. 'You're so independent, you'll go it alone rather than ask anyone for help.'

Especially me. He didn't add the last two words, but they were implied, and Lisane felt incredibly sad.

He'd make a wonderful honorary uncle. But she couldn't tell him that.

Life wasn't fair. *Love* was unfair.

'Let's go eat.'

The alfresco meal was relaxed, the fish succulent, and it was almost like old times when the four of them had shared so much.

Jean-Claude put on a few CDs, kept the music low, and when it grew dark he switched on a string of coloured lights.

This is how it could be, Lisane thought fleetingly. Family and, in the future, children. The link tying them together.

Except she wasn't part of that link.

Being with Zac had introduced her to an emotion so powerful it had become all-encompassing, primitive...like nothing else she'd previously experienced, or ever would again.

On Friday she'd take a morning flight to Brisbane and use the weekend to contact leasing agents, draft a letter of resignation...and make contact with Zac.

Even thinking about the how and when of that contact set her nerves on edge. She could, probably should have told him about her pregnancy over the phone. At least she wouldn't now be a quivering wreck at imparting the news.

'OK?'

Lisane turned and slid an arm around her sister's shoulders. 'Fine. Thanks for today, it was great to have your company.'

'Maybe tomorrow we'll take in a movie?'

She managed a smile. 'Sounds good.'

The music, the cool night breeze provided a peaceful air, and an unaccustomed weariness began to descend.

Was early pregnancy supposed to sap energy levels with clockwork regularity?

A ringing sound came from indoors, and Jean-Claude rose to his feet. 'I'll get it.'

The barbecue had long been cleaned, the dishes dispensed with, and any time soon they'd turn off the lights and retreat indoors.

It wasn't late, not long after nine unless she was mistaken, and she turned towards her sister.

'Would you like me to make tea and coffee?'

'We'll do it together.'

They rose to their feet and had only taken a few steps when Jean-Claude appeared in the doorway. His features were solemn, and his customary smile was absent.

'What's wrong?' The question fell from her sister's lips.

'Lisane. There's someone to see you.'

What? *Who?*

Then Jean-Claude stood aside, and she almost died at the sight of Zac's tall frame filling the aperture.

CHAPTER SEVEN

ZAC...*here*?

Yet there could be no mistaking the man moving towards her.

Everything seemed to have lapsed into silence. Lisane didn't hear the music, and Solene, Jean-Claude and Alain stood on the periphery of her vision as her world closed in on one man.

'What are you doing here?'

Had she just said those words? She bore no recollection of voicing them.

Zac noted her pallor, assessed the way her eyes had dilated into huge dark pools, the faint quivering of her mouth...and experienced a degree of satisfaction.

The desire to haul her in close and kiss her senseless was paramount. Except it wasn't the time or the place.

'We need to talk.' He let his gaze rove from Solene to Jean-Claude before settling on Lisane's pale features. 'We can do it here, or elsewhere. Choose.'

Alain moved forward a step, only to pause at the look Zac cast him in silent warning.

Zac's gaze speared hers, watching and divining each

fleeting emotion on her expressive features. 'Your call, Lisane.'

It was no contest. *Here* wasn't really an option. 'I'll collect my bag.' Was that her voice? It sounded almost fragile.

It didn't take long to drag a brush through her hair, apply lip-gloss and check her bag.

His hire car was parked on the street, and he unlocked the passenger door, saw her seated, then he crossed round to slide in behind the wheel.

Zac didn't offer a word as he ignited the engine and sent the car purring towards the intersection, then he headed towards the city, handling the traffic with ease.

The silence stretched interminably, and she turned her attention to the passing nightscape, idly noting the flashing coloured neon atop distant tall city buildings.

The car slowed and pulled in to the kerb adjacent to a group of shops, and indicated an Italian restaurant.

With smooth ease he slid from behind the wheel and waited until she emerged before locking the car.

'I didn't eat on the flight.'

The restaurant was well-patronised, and within minutes they were seated and handed a menu.

'Would you like something?' Zac queried as a waiter hovered close by.

'Just tea,' she accepted quietly while Zac perused the menu and gave their order.

She waited until the waiter left before speaking. 'It would have been easier to pick up the phone.'

He leant back in his chair and regarded her with deliberate appraisal.

A well-known technique designed to unsettle an opponent. For a crazy few seconds she wrestled with the feeling that was his intention, and she held his gaze, silently daring him to break it.

'Of late the phone hasn't been our best form of communication.'

His drawl held a degree of irony she chose to ignore.

The waiter delivered her tea, set down a glass of wine for Zac, then retreated out of sight.

'What made you think you could dismiss me so easily?'

Straight to the point. Well, she could play the same game.

'The shoe is on the other foot, surely?' she offered coolly, and saw the edge of his mouth tilt a little.

He didn't pretend to misunderstand. 'Allegra's ill-timed announcement to the Press.'

'Perfectly timed,' Lisane corrected. 'And deliberately designed to set the cat among the pigeons.'

An eyebrow slanted in silent query. 'Your trust in me is so tenuous?'

Was it? A week ago she'd have said *no*...but now she wasn't so sure. 'Allegra covets being Mrs Zac Winstone,' she managed with stark honesty. 'It's what her parents want.' Her pause was imperceptible. 'And yours.'

His eyes didn't leave hers, and his silence stretched until her nerves screamed in silent protest.

'They've said as much?'

Oh, his mother was too clever to put it into words, when implication worked just as well. 'No.'

'Allegra?'

In spades. 'You could say that.'

'It didn't occur to you if I wanted to marry Allegra I'd have done so by now?'

In my more rational moments.

'Or that Allegra appears to derive enjoyment in manipulating certain situations?'

Wasn't that the truth!

Her eyes sparked blue fire. 'What would you have had me say, Zac?' She was on a roll. 'It's OK with me to share you with another mistress?'

His eyes lightened with a degree of humour, and she stood quickly to her feet. 'Oh, to hell with it. This conversation isn't going anywhere.'

She turned away from him…felt the room begin to spin, then blackness descended and there was nothing.

Lisane gradually became aware of voices, and there was something cool covering her forehead. A sense of awareness rose through her level of consciousness, and her eyelids fluttered open.

Zac leant in close, his features creased with concern, and she saw two waiters hovering within touching distance.

Realisation hit…the restaurant, their argument. She'd stood too quickly…

'Lisane.'

'I'm fine.' Reassurance which didn't quite cut it.

'Sure you are.' Zac's expression darkened as he caught hold of her hands. 'I'll get you to a doctor.'

Lisane met the concern evident, and weathered it. 'I don't need a doctor to tell me what I already know.'

His eyes held hers, assessing, only to narrow fractionally. 'You're ill?'

'Not exactly.'

He went still, and she saw something sharpen in the depths of his eyes. 'You're pregnant?'

Given a choice, she'd have chosen a better time, another place. 'Yes.' She closed her eyes, then opened them again.

She made to rise to her feet, only to have Zac still her movements.

'Not so fast.' He pulled her cup and saucer close. 'Drink some tea.'

Hot, sweet, it had a soothing effect, and she watched in silence as he waved away the meal he'd ordered.

'Eat,' she protested as the waiter hovered.

A slightly hysterical laugh rose and died in her throat as Zac gave the food a cursory glance, then redirected his attention to her.

'How long have you known?'

She closed her eyes, then opened them again. 'Four days.' Days when she'd practised what she was going to say. Words that had seemed so rational for the path she'd chosen to take.

'Tell me,' Zac began carefully. 'When was I supposed to learn about my impending fatherhood?'

He was too controlled, too quiet. Like the lull before the storm.

'Or was it not part of your plan?'

Her chin lifted in silent defiance. 'How can you ask that?' Eyes as deep as sapphires blazed with anger. 'You think I should remain in Brisbane and prove an embarrassment to the Winstone family? Not to mention myself?'

'Why *embarrassment*?'

'Think of the consequences to your career, social status, and the Winstone name.'

'That's the basis for your decision?'

'Yes, dammit!'

'You don't perceive me supporting you or having an active part in our child's life?'

'My life, my child, my responsibility.'

'Our child. Our responsibility,' Zac corrected with deceptive quiet. 'We'll get married.'

For a moment she couldn't speak. 'Marriage wasn't part of our arrangement.'

'It is now.'

'I don't see marriage as *the* solution.'

'You'd deprive a child of its father? The right to feel safe and secure within a relationship with two parents, the possibility of a sibling or two? Grandparents? Consigned to the care of a nanny while you work? Having to share custody? Is that what you want for our child?'

He was good. Too good. He'd also fight tooth and nail to gain equal parenting time. With the power to make her life extremely difficult if she chose to oppose him.

'We've been together for almost a year. The only thing we haven't shared is living quarters. Why not legally formalise the relationship?'

'For the sake of the child.'

'For our future as a family.'

What about love? she agonised silently.

Didn't he realise she would never have entered their relationship if she didn't *love* him?

Yet the *l* word hadn't passed her lips…even when she'd been caught up in the depths of passion.

Zac desired her. Of that she had no doubt. But desire, emotional and physical, was a hunger of the senses. A sexual and sensual expression related to need.

Love was something else. The merging of twin souls, attuned in every way. The forever, once-in-a-lifetime kind.

A relationship could be broken.

Marriage was meant to be a lifetime commitment.

It was something she wanted. For the right reasons.

Not as a matter of convenience, because it appeared to be the right thing to do.

Was it asking too much to want the whole deal?

Would she be a fool to query if Zac would have suggested marriage had she not been pregnant with his child?

Don't go there.

Besides, you already know the answer. Why have him put it in words…words you don't really want to hear?

'Believe I'm not going away any time soon.' His voice held the deceptive silkiness of underlying determination.

Zac summoned the waiter for the bill, paid it, then he rose to his feet. 'Shall we leave?'

Lisane reached for her cellphone as they hit the pavement. 'I'll call a cab.'

He gave her a look that would have withered an adversary on the spot. 'You think I'll let you do that?'

'Why, when you're staying in a city hotel?'

'Jean-Claude offered me a bed for the night,' he relayed smoothly.

'Which you accepted.'

'You object?'

Her eyes sparked blue fire as they clashed with his. 'As long as you understand you won't be sharing mine.'

Zac unlocked the car and held open the passenger door. 'Get in, Lisane.'

The drive to Solene's home in suburban Manly was achieved in total silence, for there didn't seem to be a thing she could think of to say that wouldn't contain an element of conflict.

The house was in darkness as Zac drew the car to a halt adjacent to the pavement, and once indoors Lisane quietly turned towards the hallway…only to come to an abrupt halt as firm hands closed over her shoulders.

She barely had time to gasp a faint protest before his mouth took possession of her own in a kiss that plundered at will, conquering with the sweep of his tongue as he demanded her response.

Hungry and frankly sensual, he wove his own brand of magic until a tiny groan in capitulation sounded low in her throat, and in one simple movement she wound her arms round his neck and arched her body into the hardness of his own.

Zac slid a hand down her back to cup her bottom as he held her firmly in place, then he angled his mouth and went in deep.

Lisane had no idea how long it lasted, only that it wasn't enough. Not nearly enough as the desire for skin on skin became paramount. And need. Fast-burning need that sent her up in flames.

So much so, she whimpered in protest as he began to withdraw, easing her down with the soft brush of his lips against her own, the light, soothing movement of his hand up her back, and the gentle squeeze to the nape of her neck.

All it would take was a word, the slightest gesture, and they'd share the same room, the same bed.

She was tempted, so badly tempted it took tremendous strength of will to step back from him. The dimmed light made it almost impossible to discern his expression, and her mouth shook a little as she forced a whispered 'goodnight'.

Fingers lightly trailed a gentle path down one check. 'Sleep well.' He paused fractionally, then added with a tinge of humour, 'If you can.'

Zac watched her walk down the hallway to her room,

saw her close the door behind her, and the pencil-line of light shine beneath her door.

Frustration ran through every muscle in his body, and he fought against the desire to follow her. The image of her beautiful, silken skin laid bare tightened his erection to an uncomfortable level, and he wanted nothing more than to kiss every inch of her with tantalising slowness until she begged for his possession.

Instead he contemplated the benefits of a cold shower, only to dismiss it as he moved quietly to the room opposite the woman whose body he craved.

He wanted, *needed* to be with her. Lie with her, hold her. Convince her that marriage to him was the only solution.

His solution, he differentiated a long time later as he lay staring at the ceiling.

It would work. He'd make it work.

Because there was no other course he could conceive or accept.

CHAPTER EIGHT

LISANE drifted through the veils of wakefulness, content and secure on a subconscious level that when she opened her eyes it would be to face the familiar routine of her usual weekday.

Rise and shine, shower, eat breakfast, dress, then drive into the city to the court house.

The alarm hadn't sounded, she decided drowsily, so she had time to settle deeper beneath the covers and lapse back into sleep.

Except something brushed across her cheek, and she gave an inaudible groan as she turned her head to one side.

'Lisane.'

'Zac'?

Zac had stayed over…or was it the reverse?

Mmm, nice. She could think of nothing better than to wake in his arms and bury her lips against his warm, muscular chest, feel the touch of his hand as he trailed his fingers over her hip to trace the length of her thigh, then seek the moist heat beneath the soft, curling hair at the sensitive apex.

Early-morning sex. A great way to begin the day.

She reached out a hand, and found nothing except the coolness of an empty space in her bed.

The reality brought her fully awake and aware. Her lips parted in a soundless gasp as Zac sank down onto the edge of her bed.

He was fully dressed in a business suit, buttoned shirt and tie, clean-shaven with a Blackberry in one hand and an overnight bag at his feet.

'What are you doing here?'

He took in her tumbled hair, clear skin and examined the way her pupils dilated beneath his gaze.

'Saying goodbye before I leave for the airport.'

It was impossible not to feel a tinge of remorse. 'There was no need for you to make the trip.'

'We've already done that.'

The tiny lines fanning out from the outer corners of his eyes seemed a little deeper, so too the groove slashing each cheek. Loss of sleep? Or maybe he'd stayed up late reappraising transcripts and making notes prior to his appearance in court today.

He indicated a tray resting on the bedside pedestal. 'Solene sent in tea and toast.'

If she didn't move, she'd be fine. It was the readjustment of her body from horizontal to a vertical position that seemed to provide the necessity to rush very quickly to the bathroom.

'Thanks. I'll have it later.' After you've gone, she added silently, caught the slight quizzical twist at the edge of his mouth and knew he'd read her mind.

'I'd like you to reschedule your return flight.'

'Solene and I have plans for the rest of the week,' she managed evenly.

'Your sister is happy to change them.'

Of course she is. Anything to ease me into what she perceives as a happy-ever-after solution. 'I'll be back on Friday.'

It was a minor victory, and possibly a foolish one as Zac rose to his feet, collected his overnight bag and made for the door. 'I'll be in touch. Take care.'

Then he was out of sight, and she heard the faint murmur of voices, a door click shut, followed soon after by the sound of a car engine.

Lisane felt a strange sense of loss…which didn't make any sense. She was relieved to be rid of his disturbing presence…wasn't she?

Yet his forceful image remained in the forefront of her mind, *there*…his male scent beneath the subtle tones of his cologne almost a tangible entity, and a vivid reminder of the man himself. The extent of his power.

His marriage proposal should have thrilled her. It was what she'd secretly hoped for, yet never expected.

So why hadn't she accepted it with a joyful heart?

Because it was merely an expedient arrangement…one he'd initiated because of the child she carried.

Zac's child. A Winstone heir.

One he had every intention of claiming as his own. A child who shouldn't, by any sense of the word, have the slightest whiff of illegitimacy associated with its name.

'You're crazy,' Solene verbalised later that morning as they wandered around the Rocks area. 'What are you trying to prove?'

Sisterly honesty was nothing if not brutally blunt.

'You love him.' Solene ticked one finger off another. 'You almost *live* with him. He's one gorgeous hunk of a man. He comes from a prominent family. He's in a prestigious profession. And he's obscenely wealthy.' She lifted both hands in the air in a gesture of unaccustomed temperament. *'Hello!'*

'So I should accept his proposal with due gratitude, and be content to live my life wondering if marriage would have been offered if I hadn't fallen pregnant?'

'Oh, for heaven's sake. Get a grip on reality, why don't you?' Solene paused and turned to face her. 'You think he boarded a flight just to come talk to you in person if he didn't care?'

Lisane cast her sister a cynical glance. 'Or maybe he was just ticked off because I hung up on him and refused to take his calls?'

Solene stabbed the air in emphasis. 'Answer me this. When he discovered you were pregnant, why didn't he simply offer financial support and leave you holding the baby...literally?'

'Because it's a Winstone heir?'

'Is that what you think?'

'Dammit, I don't know what to think any more!'

'It seems to me you're bent on shooting yourself in the foot!'

'OK, so I'm a fool to want it all.' This time it was she who threw her hands up in a gesture that was part anger, part despair. 'Do you blame me for that?'

'It's what we all want,' Solene ventured quietly. 'But don't lose something worth having, just because it doesn't quite fit your expectation of perfection.' She gestured towards a nearby restaurant. 'Shall we go eat?'

Food. She seemed to be fixated on food, discovering by trial and error that some of her favoured dishes no longer suited her palate.

Consequently she deliberated over the menu, chose

something safe, then she sank back in her chair and took an appreciative sip of iced water.

'Truce?'

'Done,' Solene agreed.

Together they spent a lovely afternoon browsing the various shops, examining the crafts displayed, stopped by for flavoured ice, then they joined the stream of traffic departing the inner city for the northern suburbs.

Dinner was eaten alfresco in the cooling evening air, and afterwards they retreated indoors to watch a movie on DVD.

Zac didn't call, but then Lisane hadn't expected him to, and Solene and Jean-Claude didn't mention his name. There was a text message on her cellphone next morning, keyed in brief SMS shorthand, to which she responded in kind.

A method of communication which continued over the next few days. Days when direct calls were inadvertently missed, messages left and responses sent.

Deliberate tactics, or happenstance?

Lisane kept a smile in place and the talk light as Solene drove her to the airport on Friday morning. It was hard saying goodbye, and she felt slightly bereft as she boarded her flight.

Now that she was alone there was little she could do to still the increase in nervous tension as she drew closer to Brisbane.

She had an agenda. A list. Things to do which would ensure she kept busy until Zac called her at seven.

Busy was good. It wouldn't allow her too much time in which to think.

Three weeks' absence meant the cottage would need a clean, and somewhere in there she'd need to get in fresh food. Unpack.

Not necessarily in that order, she reflected as she disembarked at the domestic terminal and headed for the luggage carousel.

The long line of taxis made for an easy exit, and the traffic seemed less dense than its Sydney counterpart. Suburban Milton looked endearingly familiar, the cottage even more so, and she changed into cargo trousers, pulled on a T-shirt and began systematically dealing with a host of chores.

It was almost six when she unpacked the last item of food and stowed it in the refrigerator. Everything was done, except for sorting through her mail…something she'd aim to do before Zac arrived. But first, she needed to shower and change.

Zac hadn't specifically mentioned dinner. Would they eat in or out?

Lisane chose dress jeans, pulled on a singlet top and added a cropped blouse, applied light make-up and left her hair loose.

If he'd made a restaurant reservation that required more sophisticated wear, it would only take a few minutes for her to change.

She entered the lounge and switched on the television, watched for a while, then she checked the time. Seven-fifteen. Maybe he was held up in traffic.

At seven-thirty her cellphone beeped with an incoming SMS relaying an unexpected delay, and it was almost eight when a sweep of car headlights hit the front of the cottage.

Lisane had the door open before he set foot on the porch, and a tumble of words rose to the surface that failed to find voice as he anchored her face between his hands and bestowed a brief, hard kiss.

An action which temporarily robbed her of the ability to speak. Then he curled an arm over her shoulders and drew her indoors.

'Have you eaten?'

Such a prosaic question, when food was not uppermost in her mind. 'Not yet.'

'Grab your house-keys, and we'll go find somewhere close by.'

She opened her mouth, only to have him press it closed. 'Later.'

He chose a Park Avenue restaurant only a short distance away, and she waited until they were seated before querying,

'Are you going to tell me what held you up?'

An apt choice of words, Zac accorded. Except it was *who*, not what.

A gun pointed at his head, an outstretched hand, a harsh voice demanding money at a light-controlled intersection had come out without warning, and in hindsight only because he had the window wound down.

He'd had nowhere to go, trapped by cars front, back and either side. So he'd carefully reached into his jacket pocket and handed over a spare billfold filled with several hundred dollars in notes.

Then the youth had sprinted away, dodging between cars until he disappeared down a side street out of sight.

The traffic lights changed, the cars began to move, and Zac had followed through until he could pull into the nearest kerb. He had rung the police on his cellphone, then drove to the nearest police station and gave his statement.

There was the question as to whether he had been a deliberate target or simply the victim of a random act.

His field of expertise, his chosen profession lent the former a possibility the police had refused to discount.

'A slight altercation demanding my time.' Truth by omission. He perused the menu and suggested she do the same.

'You had a good flight?'

They exchanged pleasantries as they ate, polite and somewhat innocuous, given there was much to discuss.

Lisane waited until the waiter served dessert and took their order for tea and coffee before venturing carefully, 'Will you begin, or shall I?'

Zac leant back in his chair and regarded her thoughtfully. 'Cut to the chase?'

She knew the law as well as he did, and how the system worked. As father of their child, any court would grant him reasonable access and custody rights. That was a given.

Add Zac's financial status was far superior to her own…and she had no choice but to deal with it.

'I suggest we compromise.'

Her eyes sharpened a little. 'In what way?'

Zac reached for his stemmed glass and savoured the last measure of wine before subjecting her to a steady appraisal.

'We share the same residence for a month. As a prelude to marriage.'

Lisane was silent for a few timeless seconds. Was she being very cleverly manipulated…or did he really *care*?

Did it matter?

A few weeks ago she'd have agreed in a heartbeat. So what was so different now?

Don't answer that!

The waiter delivered their tea and coffee, offered a smile and departed silently.

'It's reasonable for me to want to care for you, support you through the pregnancy, the birth.'

'Don't regard me as an obligation.'

Zac wanted to shake her. Did she really think he'd give her a snowflake's chance in hell of walking away from him?

'Did I imply that?'

Being with him was what she wanted...wasn't it?

What price stubborn pride?

And what, in the name of heaven, was she afraid of?

They were going to be forever linked together because of their child. A joint united parental front was better than two separated parents living in different cities, different states.

Think of the child. Its stability and security.

'Yes.' She held his gaze with unblinking solemnity. 'I'll move in with you.'

Was he pleased? Relieved? She couldn't be sure.

'You won't regret it.'

But would *he*? she wondered.

Only time would tell.

It was after ten when Zac entered the quiet suburban Milton street and brought the Jaguar to a halt in the cottage driveway.

Nervous tension curled through her belly as he followed her indoors.

What in the name of heaven was the matter with her?

They'd been lovers for almost a year. Dammit, she'd agreed to marry him! Why *now* did she feel hesitant at the thought of sharing a bed with him? It was crazy.

Lisane made her way to the kitchen and filched bottled water from the refrigerator.

'Would you like a drink?'

She felt rather than heard him move in close behind her.

'The only thing I want—' He reached forward and plucked the plastic bottle from her hand and placed it on the bench, then he turned her round to face him '—is you.'

He cupped each cheek, then he angled his head and went in slow, brushing her lips with his own, savouring their soft fullness, felt their slight trembling and shifted a hand to hold fast her nape.

Zac took his time, wanting, needing her response, and when it came he shifted his body in close against her own and held her there, making her shockingly aware of his erection, its hard length, its power, and the anticipation of the pleasure he could gift her.

It wasn't enough, not nearly enough. He needed to touch her, caress the silken softness of her skin, and he pulled the top free from the waistband of her jeans, then slid a hand to cover one lace-covered breast. Teasing its soft fullness with the light brush of his fingers…and felt rather than heard the soft moan deep in her throat.

Her hands crept up over his shoulders and slid into the thickness of his hair as she held his head in place, and he went in deep, taking them both to a place where there was nothing else but passion…the heady desire of witching, shameless need.

With one smooth movement Zac lifted her up against him, parting her thighs so they straddled his hips, and a soft, husky sound emerged as she buried her mouth against his throat.

He carried her into the main bedroom and slid her body slowly down his own, then with infinite care he removed her top, and unclipped her bra, letting her breasts spill free.

Beautiful, their delicate peaks hard with desire as they anticipated the touch of his hands, the benediction of his mouth.

Lisane's fingers worked the buttons on his shirt, then clutched a handful of soft cotton, wrenched it free and let her mouth bestow random kisses over the tightly muscled skin at his chest.

His body jerked as she took one male nipple between her teeth and rolled it, creating a pleasure that verged towards the edge of pain.

He wanted her naked, and needy…for him, only him.

There was no reason for words, just the touch of skin on skin, the leisurely tasting that edged the passionate tension to a mesmeric, electrifying climax as he sent her high, held her there, then he entered her in one long, careful thrust that took them both to the brink, where sheer primeval sensation became a glorious rapture so intense it was almost impossible to bear.

Afterwards Zac rolled onto his back, carrying her to rest on top of him, and she buried her face into the curve of his neck, exulting in the closeness, the faint muskiness of his skin mingling with the scent of recent sex.

His hand soothed a gentle path over her spine, curved over the soft swell of her bottom, then eased up to settle at her nape.

Soon he'd shift her to lie curled in against him and they would sleep…but for now he wanted the post-coital closeness, the lingering aftermath of very good sex.

CHAPTER NINE

'I WENT grocery shopping yesterday,' Lisane protested over breakfast next morning, and wondered precisely *why*, when her shift into Zac's apartment was imminent. Common sense didn't appear to be uppermost in her mind of late.

Zac cast her an amused look as he drank the last of his coffee. 'Why not box and gift them to the city homeless shelter?'

She had no problem with that. She did, however, protest at his suggestion to call in professional packers.

'Why,' he queried reasonably, 'when it can be done in a fraction of the time and with minimum ease at your direction?'

She had household linens and towels, books, ornaments…*furniture*.

'Because I need to sort out what to take, and what can be stored.'

He stood to his feet and began clearing their breakfast dishes. 'A decision on removalists and storage can be made later.'

Zac made it sound easy. A small truck dispensed by professional packers would transport all her personal effects in one move. Whereas even with two cars it would take two or more trips.

She was, she decided ruefully, merely being pernickety. Why choose the difficult path when there was a simple one?

'OK.' Lisane gave a slight shrug in capitulation. 'Let's get it done.'

Wealth equated with power, and all it took was for Zac to make a phone call to arrange to have a husband-and-wife team arrive in an hour.

They were good, careful, very efficient, and in what seemed a very short time everything she needed to take had been packed, loaded into the enclosed truck and was ready for delivery.

Lisane ran a security check, then she collected her keys and followed Zac onto the porch.

'You leave first, and I'll follow,' he indicated as she crossed to the garage.

Why should it feel different from any other occasion when she'd driven to Zac's apartment? she pondered as she drove away from the cottage.

Except this time she wouldn't be coming back...at least not in the usual sense.

This move was a large step towards permanency.

With a view to marriage.

It was what she wanted. But not in the order it was happening.

And not, she reflected sadly as she entered the inner city, as a result of *duty* because of the child she carried.

Oh, for heaven's sake...we've been there, done that, so let's not do it again.

As Zac indicated, the transition from her cottage to his

apartment was effected with minimum effort, and within a short space of time her clothes were neatly displayed in the large walk-in wardrobe in the main bedroom, and everything else placed in drawers.

Dinner was something they sent out for and ate alfresco on the terrace as they watched the city come alive with streetlights and coloured neon while the sun disappeared beneath the horizon.

From this height everything looked so peaceful…a tranquil nightscape that never failed to entrance, despite the knowledge the city's underbelly held crime and violence.

An inevitable dark side Zac dealt with in the courtroom on an ongoing basis…as did she, to a lesser degree.

Winners and losers, Lisane contemplated. Aware that the guilty sometimes got off, while the occasional innocent was deemed guilty.

'I have something for you.'

Lisane turned towards Zac, whose profile was slightly shadowed in the reflected light spilling onto the terrace from indoors, making it difficult to gauge his expression.

She watched as he withdrew a small jeweller's box and placed it on the glass-topped table.

A protest left her lips as he opened the box, then she gave an audible gasp.

Something was an exquisite diamond solitaire that shot prisms of red and blue fire as he transferred it from the box to her finger.

'I can't accept this.'

'It's the appropriate symbolic gift.' There was a degree of humour evident in his voice.

Lisane's eyes widened with a measure of shocked pleasure. 'Anything much *less* would have been adequate.'

'No,' he responded with teasing indolence. 'It wouldn't.'

A slight frown creased her forehead. 'Zac—'

'We mutually agreed on a period of engagement, did we not?'

'Yes,' she allowed. 'But—'

'No *buts*.'

She wanted to say he was going too fast, and that a ring was too much, too soon.

'Tomorrow we're lunching with my parents,' Zac continued. 'I've also organised for an announcement notice to appear in tomorrow's newspapers.'

Oh, my.

'No comment?'

Stop the world, I want to get off, came vividly to mind! 'Do they know about the baby?'

'They're very excited about the prospect of a grandchild.'

Tomorrow *is* going to be fun. Her stomach was already staging a silent protest of its own by twisting into a nervous knot.

'Why don't you go phone Solene?'

A sisterly exchange offering a mix of congratulations— *you're doing the right thing*—commiseration—*his parents are part of the package*—and common sense—*thank heaven you've come to your senses*?

'She's on your side,' Lisane offered, and saw one eyebrow lift in a gesture of musing cynicism.

'And that's a bad thing?'

'Yes.'

Zac gave a husky laugh. 'Let's agree to disagree, hmm?'

Lisane rose to her feet without a further word, and

gasped out loud as he pulled her down onto his lap, then fastened his mouth on her own in a kiss that stole her breath.

'I'm going to run a bath.' He released her onto her feet and shaped her slender frame. 'Come join me when you're done.'

Heat surged through her body at the mere thought of sharing his ablutions, the soft, fragrant bubbles and the slow drift of his hands on her body.

'The bath water might have cooled by then.'

'You think?'

His faint chuckle sounded softly in her ear as she re-treated indoors.

Conversation with her sister was of necessity a little one-sided, given Solene and Jean-Claude were dining with his parents.

Consequently Solene's responses were restricted to 'uh-huh', 'that's great', *'really?'*, and lastly the promise to call back at a more suitable time.

Lisane cut the connection, her expression thoughtful as she moved through the luxurious apartment towards the main bedroom.

She found her eyes drawn to the ring on her hand, and she examined its purpose while endeavouring to find a balance between sheer joy and unwanted reflection.

Why the feelings of ambivalence?

A faint groan in self-castigation emerged from her throat.

It was like riding an emotional see-saw…and more than time she got off and grounded herself firmly in reality.

Zac was in the process of shedding his clothes when she entered their bedroom, and he took one look at her guarded expression, detected the warring emotions and kept his voice light.

'Not the most convenient time to talk?'

Lisane threw him a quick glance, and felt her heart execute a backward flip at the sight of the muscular symmetry of his honed body, the sleek flex of sinew apparent with every move. 'She'll call back.'

His gaze pierced hers as he unbuttoned his jeans, slid them down over his thighs and stepped out of them. Without a further word he crossed to her side and swept an arm beneath her knees, then lifted her lightly against his chest.

'What do you think you're doing?'

She missed his teasing smile as he walked towards the *en suite*.

'Zac?' Dear lord, he did intend dumping her fully clothed into the bath?

'Don't!' The plea escaped as a scandalous shriek as he held her suspended over the gently steaming bubbles. 'Please,' she added in desperation, and didn't know whether to laugh or cry as he eased her down onto her feet.

'Fool.' She curled her hand into a fist and aimed it at his shoulder, heard his soft laugh and repeated the action, only to have his mouth settle over her own in a warm, evocative kiss.

It was all too easy to link her hands together behind his neck and sink in against him. To savour the warmth of his embrace and anticipate the heat as he gently released her from her clothes.

No protest emerged from her lips as he swung her into his arms and stepped into the bath, then settled her down to sit in front of him.

The water temperature was just right, and she closed her eyes as she leant back within the cradle of his arms. A powerful thigh lay either side of her own, and a soundless sigh of pleasure remained locked in her throat as he soaped a sponge and began lightly smoothing it over her skin.

'Is it working?'

Lisane didn't pretend to misunderstand. 'You know it is.'

Right at this moment there was no need for words. They were perfectly in tune, twin halves of a whole, and nothing outside this marble-tiled steam-filled room mattered...only them, the stirring emotions beneath the slow, caressing drift of hands, the gently seeking fingers, the touch of his lips against her temple, her ear, her soft, vulnerable nape.

It was almost possible to believe the impossible...that he adored and cherished her.

She turned slightly in his arms and angled her mouth into his, then traced its contours with the tip of her tongue, ventured in and began exploring his mouth's texture.

Zac allowed her free rein, then he took control and went in deep, his possession frankly sensual...until it wasn't enough. Not nearly enough.

In one careful move he repositioned her to sit facing him, and he cradled her close as he sought the sensitive hollow at the edge of her neck, then trailed low to tantalise the soft fullness of her breast.

With an achingly slow touch he shaped her body with his hands, then he tested the weight of each breast before sliding up to cup her face.

His kiss was so incredibly gentle, she felt boneless and wholly his as need spiralled from deep within, heating her blood to fever pitch.

More, she wanted, *needed* more, and the breath became trapped in her throat as he trailed an exquisite path to the apex of her thighs, initiating an exploration of her labia before seeking the sensitive clitoris.

Lisane cried out at his touch, almost begging his fulfilment as he drove her high...so high she arched up against him, then held back a low moan as he caught the peak of one swollen breast in his mouth and began to suckle.

When she thought she could stand it no longer, he positioned her carefully and surged in deep, felt rather than heard her satisfied sigh.

Then it became her ride, her body which controlled the action...and it was he who held on, his voice a low, guttural groan as she took him high until he bucked beneath her in a primitive climax he ensured she shared.

Post-coital pleasure lingered a while, and Lisane rose from the bath, filched a towel from its rack, then she stood still as Zac took it from her nerveless fingers and began blotting the moisture from her body.

Afterwards she returned the favour, conscious of his warm appraisal of her ministrations until she was done, then he curved an arm around her waist and led her into the bedroom.

Sleep came easily, and Lisane woke next morning to the tantalising smell of freshly brewed coffee, bacon, eggs and toast.

'Rise and shine,' a masculine drawl bade with amusement, and she lifted her head to see Zac attired in a towelling robe, tray in hand.

Rising wasn't a problem. It was shining which needed some work!

'Tea and toast is supposed to do the trick.' He handed her both, then crossed round to the other side of the bed, placed the tray in a strategic position, then slid between the sheets.

She took a careful sip of tea, and followed it with a bite of toast. 'Don't take it personally if I suddenly cut and run.'

Maybe this time...maybe not, Lisane decided minutes

later as she threw on a robe and made a hurried dash into the *en suite*.

Man, she hoped this morning habit would soon change!

'Anything I can do?'

She sponged her face, and kept her back to him. 'This is one experience I'd prefer not to share.'

'Tough.'

Toothbrush, toothpaste, and within a few minutes she was done. When she turned he was still there, leaning against the doorway.

His appraisal was anything but swift, and she met his steady gaze with equanimity. 'I'm fine.'

He straightened as she drew close and stood to one side so she could pass. 'Debatable.'

'I can sleep in another room if this bothers you.'

'Not a chance in hell,' Zac stated quietly, and she threw him a dark glance.

If he dared say 'we're in this together', so help her, she'd hit him.

Breakfast in bed, or eaten out on the terrace?

The terrace won, and they sat in companionable silence, enjoying the sun's warmth as it fingered the cityscape.

Peaceful, Lisane reflected, without the rush of weekday traffic clogging the streets and the cacophony of protesting horn-blasts.

Soon she'd dress and… Her mind came to a screeching halt as reality hit. She wasn't going anywhere. She was here to stay.

And today, she remembered, they were lunching with Zac's parents.

Could she plead a malaise and opt out?

Coward, she remonstrated silently.

Felicity and Max Winstone were nice people.

Lisane was engaged to their son.

Lunch, she decided, would be a pleasant occasion…
wouldn't it?

Choosing what to wear posed a difficult decision. Smart
casual or the whole deal? And if the latter, should she opt
for the tailored office suit or something softly feminine?

She dithered, a victim of increasing nervous tension,
then muttered an unladylike oath beneath her breath and
selected a soft draped skirt in varying brown hues, added
a toning knitted top and a filmy fitted over-blouse, slid
her feet into stilettos, then tied her hair back with a
chiffon scarf.

The result was elegant boho chic, and, she hoped, *right*.

A pulse beat quickly at the base of her throat as Zac's
Jaguar turned into the established tree-lined street in one
of the city's most prestigious suburbs.

'You're very quiet.'

'I'm reserving sparkling conversation for your parents.'

'You have no need to be nervous.'

Are you kidding? *Lunch* was a whole different ball-
game from a social function meet-and-greet.

OK, you can do this, she bade silently as Zac eased the
car into the driveway of a gracious mansion set well back
from the road and came to a smooth halt outside the main
entrance.

The large double doors stood open, and Max and
Felicity Winstone appeared in the doorway, then traversed
the few steps down to the car.

Smiling, Lisane saw at once, and giving every appearance of delighted happiness.

It was, she decided minutes later, going to be all right

as she recovered from the congratulatory hugs…and the general bonhomie as they were seated in the lounge.

Max brought out champagne, and they toasted the occasion, the baby, and enquired about a wedding date.

'Soon,' Zac concurred smoothly, and incurred his mother's faint frown.

'Darling, these things take time to arrange.'

'No guest list, no media.' His voice was firm. 'Just immediate family and a celebrant.'

'But—'

'No, mother. The only decision is location.' He took hold of Lisane's hand and raised it to his lips. 'We're considering holding the ceremony in the garden at Sovereign Islands.'

They were? Since when had she agreed to a wedding *soon*?

And how soon was *soon*?

'The Gold Coast?'

'Is that a problem?'

Felicity recovered quickly. 'No, of course not. Perhaps we could host a party for you in Brisbane following the honeymoon?'

Lisane almost felt sorry for his socially conscious parent, and she turned towards Zac. 'That would be lovely, don't you think?'

She caught the faint gleam of amusement apparent before he focused attention on his mother. 'Thank you.'

Lunch was a pleasant meal eaten in the formal dining room, and afterwards Lisane offered to help clear the table…something Felicity appeared to welcome.

'We'll just stack everything on the servery,' Zac's mother declared as Lisane followed her into a large, beautifully appointed kitchen. 'I'll deal with them later.'

'It wouldn't take long,' she suggested, and received a warm smile.

'Why not? It'll give us the chance to chat.'

Depending on the subject chosen, *chat* might not be such a good idea!

'For years we thought Zac would choose the daughter of one of our dear friends.'

Uh-oh, here comes the punchline...*Allegra*.

Should she pretend to understand, or go for silence?

Silence, definitely.

'Except it didn't happen,' Felicity continued. 'Zac is very much his own man.' She offered a warm smile. 'Max and I are happy to welcome you into the family.'

You are? 'Thank you.'

Felicity began rinsing plates and transferring them into the dishwasher. 'The babe is a wonderful bonus.'

Really? 'I'm glad you think so.'

'I'd like to share in your pregnancy, if I may?'

Share as in...how?

'Help set up a nursery. Take you shopping. Fun things we can do together.'

What could she say, other than... 'Thank you'?

Felicity closed the dishwasher door and dried her hands. 'Let's join the men, shall we?'

It became a pleasant afternoon, as Felicity led them on a tour of her garden, a subject which revealed a mutual empathy with gardening, the sowing of seeds, favoured flowers and shrubs.

Max Winstone had indulged his wife's green fingers with a small glasshouse filled with beautiful orchids, which Lisane admired with genuine pleasure.

Afterwards Felicity served afternoon tea out on the

terrace, and it was almost five before Zac indicated their intention to leave.

'We'll see you Friday evening,' Felicity bade as they reached the front entrance. 'The Fabrisis' cocktail party.'

You have to be kidding.

'You hadn't forgotten?'

Could they forget...*please*?

'We intend spending the weekend at the coast.'

We do?

'We'll put in an appearance,' Zac indicated.

Oh, *good*. The cat among the pigeons? Wasn't that going to be fun!

'Not quite what you expected?'

The query came as Zac eased the car through the gates and entered the tree-lined street.

She wanted to say 'the jury is still out', except that wouldn't have been fair. She'd hold on to any reservations until after Friday evening.

'It has been a lovely afternoon.'

'Which you're relieved to have done with.'

She looked at his profile, saw the strong jawline, the sculptured facial bone structure. 'Will you hold it against me if I say "yes"?'

'Not at all. I felt much the same when I met Solene and Jean-Claude.'

'Impossible. You're the quintessential male, in no doubt as to who and what you are.'

A smile split his mouth to reveal even white teeth. 'Merely a façade.'

'Fool.'

He entered the inner city and turned his attention to ne-gotiating traffic. 'Feel like taking in a movie tonight?'

'The cinemaplex or DVD at home?'

'Your choice.'

'DVD,' she said without hesitation. 'Microwave popcorn, and an icy soda.'

'Done.'

CHAPTER TEN

LIVING with Zac lent a permanency to their relationship. The advantages were many, not the least of which being sharing so much more of his life on every level.

Lisane adored the apartment, and relished its close proximity to the inner city, for it meant she could walk to and from work each day and not have to deal with battling peak-hour traffic.

Mostly they ate in, meals which Lisane prepared, and afterwards they inevitably caught up on an overload of work.

Zac often left the apartment an hour, sometimes two, before she did in the morning…and they rarely arrived home at the same time each evening.

Twice he came to bed long after she was asleep, and she stirred at the soft drift of his hand, exulting in a leisurely, tactile lovemaking before curling in against him to sleep until morning.

Friday dawned with overcast skies and light drizzling rain. A preliminary warning as to how the evening would fare?

Lisane spent the day agonising over what to wear… whether she should go all-out in the glamour stakes, or stick with the classic little black dress.

Allegra, she knew, would excel in the latest designer wear, so why even attempt to compete?

Yet it was her first social occasion as Zac's fiancée, and, although she'd graced his arm at many soirées in the past, tonight would be different.

Even the thought set the butterflies in her stomach batting their wings in protest as she rode the lift to the penthouse apartment.

An hour. She had an hour to shower, fix her hair and make-up, then dress.

Lisane had only just entered the main bedroom when she heard Zac enter the apartment, and she slipped off her stilettos and began stripping off her outer clothes.

'Hi.'

The bright greeting didn't fool him in the slightest, and he crossed the room to her side, cupped her face between both hands, then angled his mouth against her own.

'What was that for?' she queried breathlessly as he released her, and his dark eyes gleamed with humour.

'Because I felt like it?'

'Distraction therapy.'

His soft laughter curled round her nerve-ends and tugged a little as he removed his jacket and loosened his tie.

She slipped off her tights, selected fresh underwear and disappeared into the *en suite*.

Seconds later she adjusted the temperature dial at the top edge of 'warm' and stepped beneath the stream of water.

Ten minutes to shower and wash her hair, ten minutes to shape it with the hair-drier, a similar amount of time to—

The glass door slid open and Zac stepped in beside her.

'You can't,' Lisane began as he took the soap from her hand. 'We don't have—'

'Time? Yes we do.'

He was so incredibly gentle it made her want to cry, and when he was done he collected the container of shampoo and began massaging the scented liquid into her scalp, rinsed it, then he shaped her shoulders and let one hand drift down her body, exploring each curve, the indentation of her navel, before seeking the feminine heart of her.

Skilled fingers found and stroked the sensitive nub with a touch that sent waves of sensation escalating through her body, and he caught her husky groan with his mouth in an explicit oral supplication.

She instinctively reached for him, only to have her hand imprisoned in his own.

'You can have your way with me later,' he promised, smiling as she began to protest, and he dropped a light kiss to the tip of her nose. 'Now go.'

Her body still sang from his touch as she filched a towel and used it to dry herself, before wrapping it sarong-wise round her slender form while using another to dry her hair.

Zac emerged from the shower and dried himself, then hitched the towel around his hips and disappeared into the bedroom.

It would be pleasant, Lisane decided, if they were simply dining out, instead of attending a Fabrisi cocktail party.

Something clenched inside her stomach at the thought of the evening ahead. The only positive was Zac would be at her side, and after a few nerve-racking hours spent smiling and engaging in scintillating conversation they intended driving to the Gold Coast for the weekend.

She conjured an image of his beautiful Sovereign

Islands home, their overnight bags ready to be stowed in the boot of his car…and determined to keep that image in the forefront of her mind.

The classic black dress, Lisane decided, and donned a black bra and thong. The dress was fully lined, negating the need for a slip, and she extracted new sheer black tights, pulled them on, then she slid her arms into her robe and began styling her hair with the hair-drier.

Painstaking care with her make-up brought the desired result, and she entered the bedroom to find Zac clad in black tailored trousers, pristine dress shirt, and in the process of adjusting his tie.

It took only minutes to step into her dress, close the zip fastening, then slip her feet into black stilettos.

Zac shrugged into his suit jacket as she collected her evening bag, and minutes later they rode the lift down to the underground car park.

'You look gorgeous,' he complimented, and she offered him a quirky smile in response.

'Thanks. Same goes.'

A gross understatement, she acknowledged as she slid into the passenger seat. For *he* could steal any feminine heart with effortless ease.

Was he aware of the effect he had on most women? Oh, tell it like it is…*all* women from sixteen to sixty!

He possessed the presence, the power and a primitive sensuality that promised much.

A considerable understatement, Lisane allowed silently, wondering just how many women there had been who could attest to his ability to deliver.

Focus, she commanded silently as the Jaguar joined the stream of traffic vacating the city.

Suburban Ascot encompassed prime real estate with splendid views of the city, and the Fabrisi mansion featured a stately heritage-listed property whose original owner featured high within Australian government circles.

No expense had been spared in its preservation, and it offered a glimpse into a previous century while retaining an innate graciousness their hosts took great care to maintain.

Nerves were hell and damnation, Lisane allowed as she circled the large formal lounge at Zac's side, and her eyes widened slightly as they settled on their hosts' daughter.

Tall, her sable hair beautifully groomed, Allegra looked stunning in a black fitted gown whose design hugged her toned curves to perfection.

Oh, my. This was the moment Lisane had been dreading. A face-off between the new fiancée and the woman who had assumed Zac's ring would be hers.

Perhaps it was appropriate they were both dressed in black?

Don't go there!

Did Zac have any idea of the situation he'd created?

Was it her imagination, or did the buzz of conversation suddenly become still as the guests surreptitiously observed Allegra cross the room?

Zac placed an arm along the back of her waist, and she killed the desire to lean in against him.

'Darlings.' Allegra's smile was a brilliant facsimile that didn't quite reach her eyes. 'I understand congratulations are in order.' She leaned in close and brushed her lips to the edge of Zac's mouth, lingered a few seconds too long as she pressed a hand to his chest, before she turned towards Lisane to bestow an air-kiss. 'How wonderful for you both.'

Polite was the only way to go. 'Thank you.'

'Do enjoy yourselves.' The megawatt smile was a mite overdone. 'We'll catch up again later.'

Hopefully not. Although somehow she had the feeling it was inevitable as she watched Allegra work the guests with consummate charm.

Mixing and mingling was an art form, with the exchange of air-kisses, the occasional European press of a cheek to each side of the face, a handshake, the light touch of a hand to the arm…combining greetings and small talk.

Max and Felicity Winstone arrived late with offered apologies.

'We were only a block away when the car developed a punctured tyre,' Felicity explained. 'Of all the times for it to happen.' She leaned in close and dropped a light kiss to Lisane's cheek. 'How are you, my dear?'

Max followed suit, and Lisane was grateful for the public gesture of familial solidarity.

Charmaine and Leo Fabrisi proved generous hosts, with uniformed staff presenting numerous trays of canapés and exotic-looking finger food, while waiters proffered champagne.

No special occasion, just a gathering of friends, she perceived. One of many such invitation-only evenings considered *de rigeur* on the social calendar of the favoured few.

Lisane and Zac's engagement brought voiced congratulations, and after a while her facial muscles began to ache from maintaining a constant smile.

'When is the wedding?' proved to be the most oft-asked query, and Lisane simply deferred to Zac, whose 'soon' answer brought the inevitable 'you haven't set a date yet?' response.

She would have given almost anything to drink something alcoholic to dull the edges…for, quite frankly, mineral water just didn't do it!

It was almost as if some instinctive warning mechanism had moved on to alert.

Fool, she chastised silently. Such an acute degree of sensitivity is ridiculous!

What could possibly occur in a large room filled with people…and Zac at her side?

Except a visit to the guest powder-room?

Beautifully decorated, she noted, with two individual stalls to accommodate female guests. And the only logical place Allegra could possibly stage a confrontation.

Lisane turned to face the elegantly clad young woman, and felt her heart sink.

'Allegra,' she acknowledged.

'You must think you're very clever.' The warm smile and the polite, friendly tone of voice were remarkably absent.

Oh, dear…the gloves were very definitely off. 'Is there a point to this?'

'What did you offer to get the ring, Lisane?' Allegra's eyes resembled flint as they narrowed with speculation. 'Bedroom tricks?'

She kept her gaze even. 'Why not love?'

The other woman laughed, although there was no humour in the sound. 'Oh, please. Don't insult me.'

'Are you done?'

Allegra's eyes glittered. 'Pretty little ring, darling.' Her head tilted slightly. 'Although I'd have chosen something…*more*.'

Calm. Polite. She could do both. 'It's the gift itself that's important, don't you think?'

Allegra's hands curled, and for a wild moment Lisane thought Allegra might hit her.

'Hope you don't have any secrets a close scrutiny might reveal. I doubt Zac would appreciate the media attention.' She turned and swayed towards the door, only to pause and look back over her shoulder. 'Don't count on making it to the altar.'

Where was a smart comeback when you wanted one?

The door closed behind Allegra before Lisane could think of a pithy response.

Well, now, wasn't that *fun*?

She needed a moment to compose herself before joining the guests, and she practised a smile, checked it in the mirror, only to discard it as totally fake.

Think warm and fuzzy.

A newborn baby, small and perfect, with Zac's dark hair and smile.

Better.

Just to be sure she added a touch of blusher to her cheeks and applied lip-gloss before re-entering the large lounge.

Zac was deep in conversation with an associate, and she made her way towards him.

As she reached his side he caught her hand and threaded his fingers through her own, then he absently brushed a thumb over the delicate veins inside her wrist.

'Ready, darling?'

Darling? Zac had never called her anything other than her name. Yet it appeared they were about to leave, and for that alone he deserved a stunning smile.

'Whenever suits you.'

His gaze narrowed thoughtfully as it skimmed her

features, noting the slight pallor beneath the expertly applied cosmetics, the faint shadows in those beautiful blue eyes.

Allegra?

Without doubt.

Leaving took a while as they paused to speak with his parents, before seeking their hosts, and Lisane gave a small sigh of relief as she slid into the front seat of the Jaguar.

Sovereign Islands lay a fifty-minute drive south, and they bypassed the city route and chose the gateway bridge which linked directly with the major motorway south.

The night sky was a dark indigo with a sprinkling of distant stars and a sickle moon.

It was good to lean back against the head-rest and let the tension ease from her body as she viewed the passing and opposing traffic.

'Did Allegra threaten you?'

No preliminaries, just straight to the point! Lisane didn't pretend to misunderstand. 'The word is open to interpretation.'

'As in?'

'I can assure you there are no skeletons in my family closet which could prove an embarrassment to the Winstone dynasty,' she revealed drily.

He spared her a swift dark glance and a muscle bunched at the edge of his jaw. Allegra could be a bitch, and he could well imagine her stinging verbal attack.

'I handled it.' And she had. Although she'd have given her eye-teeth to have come up with a cutting parting remark!

Lisane closed her eyes in a pretence of sleep, only for it to become a reality, and she came awake to the touch of

Zac's lips brushing her cheek…and the visual knowledge the car was stationary in the lit garage of his Sovereign Islands home.

'We're here.' An obvious statement, if ever there was one.

Zac slid out from behind the wheel, gathered their overnight bags from the trunk and led the way into the house.

A beautiful home, Lisane acknowledged with pleasure as she followed him into the main lobby.

High plastered ceilings, ivory-painted walls, with matching ivory marble tiles covering the ground floor. Modern furniture, floor-to-ceiling tinted glass along the eastern side of the house to catch the view out over the water. Formal and informal lounges, a formal and informal dining room, spacious kitchen, guest retreat and utility-rooms comprised the lower floor, with a wide curved staircase leading from the main lobby to the upstairs suites.

She had fallen in love with the place at first sight, its design and style, the magnificent view, the pool and the serenity it offered after the rush of city life.

'I'll take these upstairs.'

Lisane turned towards him with a smile. 'I'll go make a cup of tea. Will you have coffee?'

'Thanks.'

She had it ready by the time he entered the kitchen, and they took it out onto the covered terrace, where there was nothing except the water, the sky and the faint moving starboard light of a cruiser moving languidly on the bay.

The peace and tranquillity soothed her soul, and she slid off her stilettos and leant back in the comfortable lounger.

'We could take the boat out tomorrow.'

Lisane turned towards him and admired his profile in the dimmed light. Angles and planes, strong facial bone structure and a broad, loose-limbed frame possessed of whipcord strength.

'We could stop off at Couran Cove for lunch and relax there for a few hours.'

'Sounds great.' The day, the cocktail party, the drive…it was beginning to catch up with her, and she fought against the tendency to slip into a light doze.

What was it with the evening tiredness?

'Come on, sleepyhead,' Zac bade with amusement as he rose to his feet, stacked their cups together, then extended his hand…which she took and collected her shoes as she entered the house at his side.

'Go on up to bed. I'll take these through to the kitchen, then follow you.'

It was bliss to remove her outer clothes and peel off her tights, then she crossed the room to the *en suite* and began cleansing off her make-up before brushing her teeth.

Lisane reached for a covered elastic band to secure her hair, only to have Zac appear behind her and still her hands.

'Leave it loose.'

He stood head and shoulders above her, her hair so pale in contrast to his own, and she appeared positively petite in comparison to his broad frame.

A warm melting sensation crept through her body as he lifted the hair at her nape and brushed his lips to the sensitive curve beneath one earlobe.

His hands skimmed over her shoulders and deftly unfastened her bra, then slid the straps down over her arms.

All that separated her from nudity was a black silk thong, and she could almost feel her eyes dilate as he reached forward and cupped her breasts in his hands, gently shaping them until she felt the peaks harden beneath his touch.

'Zac...' It wasn't a protest, just a helpless wisp of a sigh as she watched her body bloom beneath his hands.

She could almost swear the surface of her skin tinged the palest pink as blood fed sensitive nerve-endings, and her eyes darkened to the deepest sapphire.

'This isn't fair.' The faint groan left her lips, and she felt the latent sensuality in the brush of his mouth along the edge of her shoulder, the hard ridge of his arousal as he drew her back against him.

One hand slid over her ribcage to her stomach, then splayed low as it inched beneath the thong and sought the intimate folds protecting her femininity.

Moist heat greeted his questing fingers, and she arched back against him as he leisurely stroked her, gradually increasing the intensity until she went wild in the throes of acute sensation.

Ohmigod. Was that wanton female depicted via mirrored image *her*?

She looked almost unrecognisable, her lips parted in the aftermath of ecstasy...and her eyes. Dear heaven, her eyes...

Lisane bowed her head and let her eyelids drift closed. Not in shame...but it was almost too much to witness. A secret part of herself she'd never seen, never realised existed.

'This is what I see each time we make love,' Zac said huskily. 'A beautiful young woman who is so caught up in passion it consumes her body, her soul.' He took hold of her shoulders and turned her to face him, then he tilted her chin so she had to look at him.

'My woman,' he said quietly. 'The mother of my child. Soon to be my wife.'

She lifted her arms up and clasped her hands together

behind his neck, then urged his head down towards her own and she angled her mouth into the warm heat of his in a kiss that offered him her heart…everything she was.

It would be so easy to say she loved him…would love him for as long as she lived.

Except the words remained locked in her throat as he swept an arm beneath her knees and carried her to their large bed, laid her there and dispensed with his clothes, aware she watched every move before he joined her.

Their lovemaking was leisurely, a long, sweet tasting that inched the sensuality high until only the physical coupling would suffice, and she cried out as he entered her in one long thrust, then clung as she enclosed him, becoming lost as he took her high, so high the muscular spasm of multiple orgasms shook her slender frame.

Afterwards he held her close, and she drifted to sleep in his arms.

Breakfast was something they cooked together and shared out on the terrace. There was no hurry to do anything, and they read the Saturday-morning papers, then Lisane tidied the kitchen while Zac went down the jetty to inspect the cruiser.

It was a beautiful summer's day, the skies blue with barely a drift of cloud and the sun warm with the promise of fine weather.

Lisane packed cold drinks into the cooler, added fruit, then she collected a hat, sun-screen cream, and was ready when Zac returned indoors.

Shorts and a top was suitable wear, with a sweater draped over her shoulders, its sleeves loosely knotted beneath her throat. Joggers on her feet, sunglasses pushed high on her head.

Zac wore similar apparel, and she looked silently askance as he collected the cooler.

'No problems. Let's go.'

The sea was smooth, with only the slightest breeze to ripple its surface as Zac headed out towards the open harbour, *en route* to Couran Cove.

They passed so many mansions sited on the seven linked islands comprising suburban Sovereign Islands. Almost every island was built on, magnificent multi-million-dollar homes on various canal- and bay-front land. Prestigious, expensive and luxurious, there were boats and cruisers moored at almost every jetty.

Palm trees lined the streets, and residential gardens bore flower borders, topiary and sculptured fountains, beautiful bird-baths, scrupulously maintained by an army of professional gardeners and landscapers.

Zac headed the cruiser towards open waters and made steady speed to a tourist island almost forty-five minutes distant.

The air was fresh with a brisk ocean breeze, and as they drew close a string of villas was apparent set against the background of rainforest.

Private craft were moored at the jetties, and a number of tourists were on a day trip to enjoy what the island offered.

Lisane found it fun to ride the island 'train' around the various carriageways where bush-chalets nestled in seclusion, and she took Zac up on his suggestion to lunch at the oceanfront restaurant.

Through the plate-glass windows lay the numerous sand-hills, spinifex, and the Pacific Ocean, whose blue waters stretched far out to the horizon as they sparkled and dappled beneath the midday sun.

Fine food, a relaxed ambience... Pleasant, she determined, to share time with him without needing to rush anywhere.

Here, dressed in casual attire, he didn't look the hard-hitting criminal lawyer of high repute who possessed a verbal repertoire second to none.

Lisane saw him lift an enquiring eyebrow, and her mouth curved into a musing smile.

'I'm trying to decide who you might be if you weren't *you*.'

His faint laughter curled round her heart.

'And what have you come up with?'

She tilted her head to one side, and her eyes assumed a slightly wicked sparkle. 'Nothing seems to fit.'

He finished his coffee, withdrew his wallet and paid the bill. 'Shall we leave?'

They rode the 'train' part-way and chose to tread the winding track through the lush rainforest to the harbour.

'Thanks,' Lisane said with sincerity as they boarded the cruiser.

'For what, specifically?' Zac queried as he started up the engine and began easing the craft away from the jetty.

'The weekend,' she elaborated simply. 'Today.'

'It's a pleasure.'

It was almost five when he secured the cruiser at Sovereign Islands, and Lisane went on up to the house while he shut everything down.

A shower was a priority, for there was salt-spray in her hair, on her skin, and she needed to wash off the sun-screen cream.

Zac entered the *en suite* as she emerged from it, and she pulled on dress jeans, added a knitted top, then she secured her damp hair into a pony-tail. Moisturiser, lip-gloss, and she was done.

'Want to eat in or go out?'

Zac strolled into the bedroom with a towel hitched at his hips.

He was something else. Strongly muscled torso, admirable breadth of shoulders, and possessed of an intrinsic sensual sexuality that melted her bones every time she looked at him.

'In,' she said at once. 'I'll cook.'

He pulled on underwear and stepped into jeans. 'There's steak in the refrigerator. I'll set up the barbecue.' He reached for a polo shirt and dragged it on. 'You fix a salad.'

Just as they were about to eat there was a light shower of rain, which meant transferring their meal indoors.

Afterwards Zac slotted a DVD into the player and settled down onto the sofa with Lisane curled close against him.

A romantic comedy, it had laugh-out-loud moments, and the last thing she remembered watching was a stay-at-home dad trying to cope with a toddler, a rebellious four-year-old and a dog which had somehow slipped into the house and was creating mayhem.

She was unaware of Zac lifting her into his arms and carrying her to bed, and she barely stirred when he carefully divested her of her clothes and slid her into bed.

It was morning when Lisane woke, and late, she determined with a swift glance at the bedside clock, and she rose gingerly into a sitting position, then patted her stomach and bade it *behave.*

Minutes later she cautiously slid from the bed and made it into the *en suite* without having to break into a run.

Could this be the beginning of the end of morning sickness? If so...yahoo and hallelujah!

It was impossible to suppress a grin as she dressed in jeans and a cropped top, and it became a delighted smile as she went downstairs to the kitchen, collected a bowl and added muesli and fruit, then carried it out onto the terrace.

Zac was seated at the outdoor table, coffee in hand, and he glanced up as she approached.

'Hi.'

'You should have woken me.'

The warmth of his smile sent spirals of sensation curling through her body as he reached forward and drew out a chair for her. 'Why?'

'It's too nice a day to spend any of it in bed.'

'I thought we might drive into Surfer's Paradise and take a walk along the beach.'

Lisane wrinkled her nose at him. 'You're indulging me.'

'You don't want to be indulged?'

'You're kidding me?'

Bliss, absolute bliss, she decided an hour later as they trod the sandy foreshore adjacent to the esplanade, where high-rise apartments dominated the skyline.

Fresh air carrying the tang of the sea on a soft breeze beneath the summer sun. What could be more inviting?

Walking hand-in-hand with a lover as they strolled along the broadwalk?

Relaxing over a café latte at a pavement café and watching the people walk by?

All of that, and more, Lisane decided as she became lost to introspection of the deep and meaningful kind.

She had earned Zac's respect and affection. He would,

she knew, ensure she was well cared-for and gift uncon-
ditional love to their child.

It was enough.

Wishing for the moon and the stars in the love stakes
was the stuff of dreams, not reality.

He was insisting on marriage, permanence.

It was what she wanted…so what was the problem?

'Pleasant thoughts?'

Zac's musing drawl intruded on her self-analysis, and
she offered him a slow, sweet smile.

'Yes.'

'Do you intend to share?'

Her smile widened. 'No.' Her eyes assumed a mischievous gleam. 'You might get a swelled head.'

The edge of his mouth twitched a little. 'Let's move
on and have lunch.' He withdrew a note from his wallet
and signalled the waitress, paid for their coffee, then he
rose to his feet and caught hold of her hand as they walked
to the car.

Tedder Avenue at Main Beach was a perfect choice, and
she gave him a delighted smile as he eased the Jaguar into
a parking space.

'You really know how to indulge a woman.'

'Taking you to lunch?'

She waited a beat. 'That, too.'

Zac trailed light fingers along the edge of her jaw. 'An
admission, Lisane?'

He had to know the effect he had on her. All it took was
a look, the touch of his hand…and she melted.

I love you.

Her lips parted as the words rose from her throat and
lingered unvoiced on the tip of her tongue.

For a heart-stopping moment it seemed as if the world stood still, and she couldn't move.

Her eyes seemed locked with his, and she felt her mouth tremble as he traced their outline.

She lost all sense of time and place, and her pupils dilated as he angled his mouth to her own in a kiss that was little more than a light brush of his lips before he raised his head.

'Food, hmm?'

There was a teasing quality to the afternoon, an anticipation of something magical just beyond her reach. A promise she chose not to analyse or examine too closely for fear it might only exist in her imagination.

They concluded a magnificent day with dinner at an Italian restaurant overlooking the nearby marina, and it was close to midnight when they reached Sovereign Islands.

Early tomorrow morning they'd drive to the Brisbane city apartment, change into the obligatory business suits, and join their working colleagues.

But tonight…they had what remained of the night, and a leisurely loving that became a sensual supplication of the senses.

CHAPTER ELEVEN

THE morning sun held the pleasant warmth of an early summer, with barely a few wisps of soft white cloud drifting beneath the clear blue sky.

It held the promise of a beautiful day, Lisane predicted as she entered the court-house and took the lift to a suite of offices on an upper floor.

The weekend at the Gold Coast had been relaxing and a lovely break after a hectic week, both work-wise and socially.

Now, however, it was back to work with a vengeance, with the usual investigative process involving phone calls, consultations and one minor paperwork snafu which required correction.

The new girl was still finding her feet, for which Lisane made allowances. Tact and diplomacy worked well, but this was the second time the identical mistake had occurred. Which led to a suspicion the lauded praise listed in her CV might not be entirely accurate.

Consequently it was a relief to take a lunch break at her favoured café, and she bought a magazine at the news-stand *en route*, ordered, then chose a pavement table.

Herbal tea, divine food, fresh air and sunshine…who could ask for anything more?

An interesting magazine article held her attention for its hard-hitting exposure, and she glanced up as a man pulled out a vacant chair at her table.

'You don't mind if I share?'

There were a few empty tables, and a slight frown creased her forehead. She kept her voice light. 'There are other tables.'

Middle-aged, perhaps close to fifty, short cropped hair, attired in well-worn jeans and T-shirt, he didn't appear to pose much of a threat.

'What man would choose to sit alone when he can share time with a beautiful young woman?'

She couldn't help feeling mildly irritated as he rested both arms on the edge of the table, and she merely offered a polite smile before returning her attention to the magazine.

'Nice day.'

Conversation? She really didn't want to do conversation!

'Don't want to be interrupted, do you?'

Oh, heavens. 'Not particularly,' she managed quietly.

'Your life is on track.' He indicated the expensive ring on her finger. 'Nice.'

The hair on the back of her neck began to prickle as instinct provided caution.

'My son's life is ruined because of your fancy man.'

Stand up and leave. Now.

His eyes dulled and became hard. 'Don't move.' He moved one hand sufficiently for her to see a switch-blade resting beneath it. 'Saw your picture in the paper.' His lips parted slightly. 'Been watching out. Figured it was just a matter of time before I got you on your own.'

There was traffic, people walking by. She wasn't alone. There were police on patrol in the mall. A security guard on duty outside a nearby bank. Maybe she could attract their attention…

'I'd be able to hurt you and disappear in the crowd before either one of them got here.'

True, but if he thought she was just going to react like a frightened wimp, he had it wrong. 'A judge would have convicted your son on evidence—'

'Dug up by your devious lawyer boyfriend.'

Keep talking, a silent voice bade. 'Tell me about your son's case.'

'Don't start with the psycho-babble. I know all the angles.'

No, you don't. But she couldn't say that. 'Did your son's representative lodge an appeal?'

'Didn't work.'

Just as she'd thought. 'I'm sorry I can't help you.'

'You think I don't know what you're up to? Keep talking, try to get me onside in the hope I'll let you go?' His mouth thinned. 'Forget it.'

'How long will it take before our presence draws the waiter's attention? Tables are filling,' she pointed out, thankful it was true.

'You haven't finished your lunch.'

Lisane looked at the food remaining on her plate. Like she was hungry? Although the teapot held more than one cup. Maybe…

With slow movements she reached for the teapot and refilled her cup, then she lifted it with both hands and took an appreciative sip.

Don't hesitate. *Now.*

In one swift action she tossed the contents of her cup in his face, rose to her feet and ran.

She was vaguely aware of his startled yelp, followed seconds later by something sharp hitting her shoulder. Someone shouted, a table crashed and she fell to the pavement.

Most ungainly and inconvenient. She tried to stand... and couldn't quite make it.

Why, for heaven's sake?

There were people moving around her, a woman crouched down beside her. 'Just sit quietly. Someone is ringing for an ambulance.'

Why an ambulance?

It was then she saw the blood. And glimpsed the switch-blade embedded in her upper arm. Almost on cue she became aware of the pain.

How could she feel slightly dazed, yet be acutely aware of her immediate surroundings? It didn't make sense.

Her tights were ruined. One stiletto was scuffed. And as for her jacket...

She tried to check her watch and almost blacked out at the pain.

OK, so she wouldn't be going in to work this afternoon. She should phone in...

'An ambulance is on its way. You're going to be fine.'

There was one burning question. 'Did they get him?'

An answer in the affirmative meant her action hadn't been in vain.

From then on in everything happened quickly. The police arrived, followed minutes later by the ambulance.

An injection worked effectively and the pain began to subside a little as details were recorded.

By the time she reached hospital sedation had kicked in and she was feeling drowsy.

The last thing she remembered was being wheeled into Theatre…

Lisane could hear low, muted voices, and someone was doing something to her arm.

Where was she?

Submerged in her subconscious, or emerging into reality?

Her eyelids drifted open and she discovered she was in a room with pale cream walls, a television set mounted high, and there was a nurse intent on taking her blood pressure.

'Good girl. You're awake.'

In slow motion it all came flooding back. Lunch, man, the attack, police, ambulance.

Hospital, she was in hospital.

Her arm felt cumbersome swathed in a bandage and resting in a protective sling.

'I'm pregnant.' Somehow that seemed more important than anything else.

'Baby's fine, dear.'

Well, of course it is. Her arm had nothing to do with the tiny foetus in her womb.

For some reason that made her smile.

'Lisane.'

She recognised the voice and turned her head to see Zac standing close to her bed.

His features appeared relaxed, but there was something apparent in the depths of those dark eyes she chose not to examine too closely.

'How long have you been here?'

He had instant recall of the initial phone call transferred to his chambers. How he'd left instructions to postpone the afternoon's schedule before taking the lift down to his car and driving at speed to the hospital. Agonising at just how bad it could have been, and barely able to contain his rage that it had happened at all.

He'd demanded the best surgeon, a private suite… pacing up and down the corridor until the surgeon emerged from Theatre with news. Waiting impatiently while she was in Recovery before she was transferred to this suite.

Aware just how shaken up he was beneath the calm, cool exterior he managed to exude with seeming ease.

Zac bent down and brushed his lips to her cheek. 'A while.' He took hold of her hand and enfolded it in his own. 'How do you feel?'

Her eyes widened a little. How *did* she feel?

Thirsty. Not quite with-it. A little pain, some discomfort.

Safe, she decided, now that he was here.

'OK,' she managed cautiously, and swivelled her head towards the nurse. 'What's the damage?'

'The blade touched the bone, but didn't splinter it, and you have a deep flesh wound.' The nurse checked the drip, wrote something on the file, then attached it to the base of the bed, offered Zac a curt nod and left the room.

Lisane swallowed the sudden lump in her throat, and aimed for some light humour. 'It could have been worse.'

Just how much worse was something she preferred not to contemplate.

Zac pulled up a chair and sank into it, his expression carefully enigmatic as he leant towards her.

'I guess you want chapter and verse,' she offered before he had a chance to say a word.

'When you feel up to it.'

'I'm not exactly at death's door.'

The fact she could have been almost brought him undone. Even now his gut twisted painfully at the thought of how close he'd come to losing her.

'You don't need to stay,' she managed quietly.

He caught her hand and carried it to his lips. 'Trying to get rid of me?'

'Didn't you have an important meeting scheduled for this afternoon?'

'Postponed until further notice.'

'But you—'

He pressed her lips closed, and his mouth curved into a faint smile. 'Quit while you're ahead, hmm?'

Too much. He was way too much for her to cope with right now, and she felt her eyelids flutter a little as she fought the tendency to close them.

No doubt due to the after-effects of the anaesthetic, she decided drowsily as she slipped into a light doze.

When Lisane woke the room was bathed in electric light and the curtains at the window were closed.

What time was it?

From habit she checked her wrist, and found it bare. Her ring was also missing...

'I have them.'

Zac rose from the chair and extracted an envelope from the breast pocket of his jacket.

'You're still here?'

What a silly question...of course he was here, she could see him, couldn't she?

He lifted her left hand and slid the beautiful solitaire in place, then he attached her watch.

This close he had a strange effect on her breathing, and she was suddenly aware of the subtle tones of his cologne, the sensual pull as he leant in.

At that moment he turned his head and caught the expression evident in her eyes, and for a millisecond he didn't say a word, then he lifted both hands and cupped her face.

His lips grazed hers, lingered, then opened to meet her own as he savoured the sweetness of her mouth.

Lisane wanted to hold him there, to deepen the kiss to something more. Except he monitored the pace, kept it relatively light, then gently broke free.

'Where were we?' she managed breathlessly, and heard his soft laugh.

'Before you fell asleep?' he teased. 'Or just now?'

It delighted him to see the soft tinge of colour creep over her cheeks. He lifted a hand and brushed a tendril of hair back from the edge of her neck, then buried his lips in the sensitive curve.

Every nerve-cell came sensually alive as piercing sweetness surged through her body, and her mouth trembled slightly as Zac lifted his head.

A husky imprecation sounded low in his throat, and his eyes locked with hers.

'I'll alert the nurse you're awake. She suggested you might like something light to eat.'

Food. Now that she thought about it, she did feel hungry, and she ate the soup, the small omelette, and enjoyed the small dish of cantaloup and yoghurt.

'Better?'

Lisane inclined her head as the nurse reappeared and

topped up the painkiller in her drip, checked her vital signs, then disappeared.

'I've seen the police report.'

She knew the procedure. The police department would send someone in to take her formal statement, followed by a routine chain of events which would finally end in the court-room.

'When can I come home?'

Not the Milton cottage. Zac's apartment.

Since when had she begun to think of it as *home*?

'Tomorrow, all being well.' His eyes darkened fractionally. 'You won't return to work for at least a week. Understood?'

The injury was to her left arm. 'I'm sure I could manage.' Heavens, she could take and make phone calls, use her right hand for the laptop, and arrange client appointments.

'No.'

'Zac—'

His eyes hardened. 'It's not negotiable, Lisane.'

'You can't—'

'I could have lost you.'

There was something in his voice, barely beneath the surface of his control, that halted anything else she might have said.

'So,' he added with gentle silkiness, 'bear with me on this.'

Why did she suddenly feel as if she was on the verge of taking hold of something just beyond her grasp?

The air between them was suddenly electric as everything in the room faded. There was only the man, a heightened awareness, and something raw and primitive existent that almost tore the breath from her body.

It was then the nurse entered the room, and she took one look at the patient and pursed her lips.

'Mr Winstone, your fiancée needs to rest.' There was mild reproof evident in her voice. 'I suggest you take a meal break. Visiting hours conclude at eight.'

For a moment there appeared to be a silent battle of wills, which, despite the Winstone influence and wealth, the nurse intended to win.

'You're right, of course,' Zac conceded. He leant forward and cupped Lisane's cheek in the palm of his hand, then traced her mouth with his thumb. 'I'll be back in an hour. Is there anything you need?'

'A brush for my hair. Toothbrush and toothpaste.' She paused. 'Some fresh clothes to change into for tomorrow.'

'Done.'

Lisane leant back against the nest of pillows when he left and mentally replayed the past few minutes, examining not so much his words, but their implication.

He'd sounded as if he cared. A lot.

Maybe she'd take courage in both hands and ask him.

Again, maybe not.

The nurse returned, removed the drip, checked her temperature and blood pressure, and handed out two painkillers.

For a while she channel-surfed the in-room television until drowsiness overcame her and she slipped into a deep sleep, unaware of Zac's return, or how long he stayed with her.

Pain woke her through the night, and from then on she dozed and woke at regular intervals until dawn when the early-morning hospital routine kicked in.

Discharge was granted later in the day, and she was dressed and waiting when Zac walked into her suite.

His gaze skimmed her features, noted the shadows beneath her eyes, and dropped a light kiss on her cheek.

'How's the pain factor?' He brushed a hand down the length of her spine and let it rest at her waist. 'The nurse reported you had a disturbed night.'

'Bearable.' She refused to own up to anything more. Not that he was fooled in the slightest.

'I don't think another twenty-four hours here would do any harm.'

'Please. I'm taking painkillers.' She lifted a hand in an expressive gesture. 'Hospital, or at home…what's the difference?'

They drew abreast of a bank of lifts. 'As long as you understand one false move and I'll have you back here before you can turn around.'

The warning brought a faint smile as they rode the lift down to ground level. 'OK. Point taken.'

'I could have called a cab.' Lisane kept the protest light as they passed through Reception to where his Jaguar was parked illegally immediately outside the hospital entrance.

He shot her a piercing look. 'You think I would have agreed to that?' He used a modem to disarm the car's security system and opened the passenger door.

She slid into the seat and unconsciously held her breath as he leant in to fasten her seat belt.

Why did she feel so vulnerable around him? It was like being on an emotional roller coaster…crazy. Worse, it seemed, since pregnancy hormones had kicked in.

Maybe silence was a safer option, she mused as Zac eased the powerful car into the stream of traffic and headed towards the inner city.

Entering the penthouse apartment was heaven, for she

loved its spacious rooms, the clean lines of the design and decor, with its panoramic view over the city, the meandering river to the hills way in the distance.

An apartment high in the sky, part of the city, yet removed from it with the benefit of restaurants, shops, all within walking distance, parks, entertainment.

Lisane crossed the lounge to the expanse of floor-to-ceiling tinted armoured glass and drank in the cityscape, doubting she could ever tire of the view or take it for granted.

'Lost in thought, or simply admiring the view?'

She turned her head slightly as Zac came to stand beside her. 'Both, I guess.'

He placed an arm along the back of her waist. 'Want to share?'

What would his reaction be if she said *I love you*?

Even one second's hesitation in his response would tear her apart.

Did the all-consuming, everlasting kind of love exist in real life? Or were there degrees of love where two people could successfully co-exist on different emotional levels?

Was it too much to hope Zac might feel the same way about her…as she did for him?

Did it really matter?

In her heart of hearts, the answer had to be *yes*.

She needed to be wanted for herself, not because she was carrying his child.

The fact he intended to make a life with her should be enough. There were those who would consider her insane to want it all, when she had so much.

Except this apartment, his Gold Coast mansion, everything he owned…they were only material possessions.

It was the man himself, his values and beliefs that mattered. And above all, his love.

At what point did a man and a woman declare their love for each other? Not the empty, meaningless words uttered in a moment of passion. The genuine, emotion-filled expression of true, everlasting love.

Who, she wondered a trifle sadly, possessed sufficient courage to lay bare their heart…*first*?

Zac's hand slowly traversed her spine and came to rest at her nape. 'You're very quiet.'

Because I'm terrified and afraid…and so incredibly emotionally mixed-up, it's crazy!

Steps, Lisane reflected.

Isn't life all about taking steps?

Even small steps result in progress…in one direction or another. And how was she going to know in which direction she was going unless…?

'Do you have any idea what I went through when I heard you'd been injured?' Zac queried huskily as he carefully turned her within the circle of his arms.

She looked at him, and became mesmerised by the darkness evident in his eyes.

'Your child is safe.'

Something moved in those dark depths, and she couldn't look away. 'You think the child you carry is my only concern?'

Isn't it?

A soft imprecation emerged, pithy, emotive and emitted with restrained vengeance.

Her eyes widened at the silent anger evident in his expression, and for a wild moment she thought he might physically shake her.

Tears welled, shimmered and threatened to spill beneath his intent gaze.

'It would have been easier if…' she began, and faltered to a halt, unable to say the words.

'You miscarried? For whom? You?' Zac demanded in a harsh, almost ravaged voice.

No, she longed to scream. *You.*

'You can't deny the pregnancy has caused complications.'

'How so?'

Oh, heavens, why hadn't she just shut her mouth? 'We shared a pleasant relationship,' she began unevenly. 'A mistaken pregnancy wasn't meant to form part of it.'

'You regard the conception of our child as a mistake?'

Oh, hell. She should know better than to parry words with the maestro of verbiage. 'Unexpected and un-planned,' she clarified.

'But not unwanted.'

How could it be otherwise? A child in Zac's image. A darling little dark-haired boy with big dark eyes and a gorgeous smile.

'No.'

Was she so steeped in tradition? Did it really matter if the conception of a child came before marriage?

Not if *love* was the main criteria.

Yet she didn't even know if what he felt for her was anything other than fondness and affection.

Was either emotion a strong enough foundation for marriage?

Sadly, she didn't know.

'What do you think will change when we marry?'

When not *if*. Lisane noted the difference. 'Marriage should be for ever.'

'You perceive ours won't last?'

He was good at this. Too good. 'How can it?' she said simply.

'Perhaps you'd care to explain your reasons why?'

'Dammit, we're not in a court-room!'

'No,' he agreed with brooding savagery. 'Otherwise I'd verbally tear you to pieces.'

'So what's stopping you?'

Zac cupped her face and bent his head down to hers. 'This.' Then his mouth was on hers in a possession that transcended anything he'd bestowed on her before.

Riveting and evocative, it was raw, primitive and passionate. Taking more than she could give in a ravishment so shamelessly intense, she uttered a faint moan in protest.

Lisane felt the moment he sensed it, and she gave a choked sigh as his mouth softened into a slow, sensual supplication that fragmented her senses and wreaked havoc with her emotions.

A tear spilt down her cheek, touched his mouth and was followed by another.

She closed her hand into a fist and hit his shoulder in a punitive effort as he slowly eased to a gentle, evocative tasting until her lips trembled beneath his own.

When he lifted his head she could only look at him with dark eyes bruised with emotion, and he pressed his lips against each eyelid in turn.

'*You*,' he vowed quietly. 'Only you.'

Lisane opened her eyes and met his own. Then almost died at the expression evident. Naked passion…and something more, so much more.

'The knowledge you carry our child is a wonderful gift. For both of us. One I would never deny,' he added gently.

'But it is you who matter to me more than anyone or anything in this world. You're the love of my life. Everything.'

Zac watched her face transform as the impact of his words registered. The joy, *love* evident in her beautiful blue eyes…for him.

'Without you,' he said gently, 'there is no light, no warmth. Nothing.'

He'd never said, not once…

'How could you not know?' His voice was husky with emotion. 'Every time we made love…it was with my heart, my soul. All that I am.' He paused imperceptibly. 'For you. Only you.'

A faint smile tilted the edges of her mouth. 'And I thought it was just good sex,' she teased, and gasped as he caught her lower lip between his teeth, nipped a little, then released it.

'Minx.' He laughed softly.

Her eyes gleamed and almost danced with mischief. 'Hmm, maybe I will marry you, after all.'

His eyes held hers, no longer light, but strangely serious. *'Because?'*

Her expression sobered. 'I love you.' The words came from the depths of her heart. 'I always have. From the very beginning,' she said quietly, adding, 'Otherwise I wouldn't be with you.'

Zac rested his forehead against her own. 'Thank you.'

His warm breath teased the loose hair at her temple, and he gently tucked the wayward lock behind her ear.

'Tomorrow we'll go down to the coast for a few days.'

She moved her head to look at him. 'Tomorrow? But you have a busy schedule. Aren't you due in court on Friday?'

His smile almost undid her. 'Postponed and rescheduled.'

'Oh.'

'There's more.'

'As in?'

'A wedding.'

'Whose?'

He pressed a light kiss to the tip of her nose. 'Ours.'

She couldn't think of a suitable word, and he touched a finger to her lips.

'This weekend.'

'But you can't—'

'An intimate family wedding in the garden of our Gold Coast home.'

'It isn't possible to arrange—'

'My parents, Solene and Jean-Claude.'

A very private ceremony. 'Really?' No fuss, no media, just immediate family and a celebrant.

'Really.'

Her eyes lightened to a brilliant cerulean blue. 'Saturday?'

'Uh-huh.'

Oh, my.

'Everything is organised.'

'I think maybe I should sit down.'

His soft laughter sent warmth fizzing through her veins, and she laid her head into the curve of his shoulder, exulting in his clean male scent beneath the subtle tones of his cologne.

'Go do that,' Zac bade as he gently put her at arm's length. 'Connect with Solene while I put a meal together.' He glimpsed the unasked question on the edges of her lips. 'And no, I didn't enlighten her about the assault.'

That meant she could keep it light and downplay the details.

'Half an hour, OK?' He trailed light fingers down her cheek, and his smile almost melted her bones. 'We eat, then you get to rest in bed.' He touched a finger to her parted mouth. 'Doctor's orders.'

Did happiness transcend physical pain? It seemed that way, for her wounded arm was the last thing on her mind as she talked with Solene, whose excitement almost matched her own.

The wedding arrangements took precedence as they discussed apparel, flowers, the ceremony itself, exchanging ideas.

'There's just one other thing,' Lisane added, and gave a brief outline of the assault.

'My God.' Solene's dismayed concern hit home. 'Are you all right? This happened *yesterday*. And you're only telling me *now*. Put Zac on the phone.'

'He's in the kitchen—'

'Preparing dinner? Which means you can't. Put him on the phone.'

'There's no need to fuss—'

'You're my baby sister. I can fuss all I like, and I will until I get some answers.' There was a second's silence. 'If I don't get them, I'm on the next flight. Bank on it.'

Lisane walked into the kitchen, caught Zac's raised eyebrow and offered him the hand-held phone. 'Solene.'

He calmly answered the questions Solene obviously shot at him in rapid succession, and from what Lisane could tell he easily dealt with each and every one of her sister's concerns before he solemnly handed back the phone.

'OK. I'm convinced. Just be warned I want all the details at the weekend.'

'Got it.'

'Now go eat, and take care.'

'Yes, ma'am.'

'I'm so happy for you.' Solene sounded as if she was close to tears. 'Love you heaps.'

'Same goes.'

Lisane cut the connection, and watched as Zac served pasta onto two plates, added the sauce, and took herbed bread from the oven.

'Go take a seat.'

It was a delicious meal, and she said so, then attempted to kill the tendency to yawn as tiredness began to descend. The pain in her arm had moved up from a persistent niggle to a nagging ache.

'Let's get you settled in bed,' Zac declared as he noted her pale features and dilated eyes.

'I can manage.' A useless protest he ignored as he carefully divested her of her clothes, gave her bathroom time, then saw her nestled against a bank of pillows in their large bed.

He operated a module which automatically opened cabinet doors exposing a television set, switched it on, then handed her the remote.

'I'll be back in a few minutes.'

He returned in five minutes with tea and painkillers, ensured she took the latter, then he stretched out beside her and locked his hands behind his head.

'Thanks.'

His eyes met hers, and he had to wonder if she had any idea what she did to him, or the power she held with her loving smile.

It was the smile that melted his heart every time, for it seemed to come from deep inside, radiating to her eyes, almost liquidising those lovely blue depths with an emotion so expressive it was all he could do not to pull her into his arms and kiss her senseless.

More, much more. To slowly bare her skin, and embrace every inch of her with his lips, to succour and tease, take her to the edge of sensual fulfilment, then hold and join her in a glorious mutual climax before sharing the free-fall.

To think he might have lost her…

His eyes hardened, and his heart turned to stone. The man who assaulted her would pay, and pay dearly. If the switch-blade had entered her body mere inches to the right, he'd be making arrangements for her funeral, not their wedding.

'You don't need to stay with me.'

Zac slowly turned his head towards her and reached for her hand. In seeming slow motion he brought it to his lips, and she almost died at the expression evident in those dark eyes.

'Yes,' he managed quietly. 'I do.'

Everything she'd ever wanted, hoped and longed for was right here.

Love. The enduring, everlasting kind.

A gift so infinitely precious, it was beyond price.

Emotion filled her until it became almost more than she could bear, and her mouth shook a little as moisture welled in her eyes.

Dammit, she wasn't going to cry.

'Don't,' Zac chastised gently, and she managed a trembling smile.

'I didn't think it was possible to be so happy.'

His eyes held hers. 'Believe that's not going to change.'

He'd make sure of it.

All the days of his life.

It was a while before he sensed her breathing begin to deepen, and long after she fell asleep he eased himself from the bed, shed his clothes, then carefully slipped in between the covers to lie at her side.

She needed to rest, and he wasn't going anywhere soon.

EPILOGUE

'READY?'

'Yes,' Lisane said simply.

Within minutes she'd descend the curved staircase at Solene's side and walk outdoors into the garden, where Zac stood waiting for her in the presence of his parents, Jean-Claude and the celebrant.

'You look beautiful,' Solene complimented with genuine sincerity as she leant in close and touched Lisane's cheek with her own. 'There are so many wishes…' she trailed gently. 'I'll settle on one. May you be as happy for the rest of your life as you are today.'

'You're going to make me cry if you say anything more.'

'Don't you dare,' her sister admonished.

The past few days had passed with a dreamlike quality, Lisane reflected, for Zac had organised everything with admirable ease.

Within an hour of their entering his Sovereign Islands home on Wednesday morning, a bridal consultant had arrived with a large folder of dress designs and material swatches, from which Lisane chose a simple gown in ivory silk. Ivory roses were the flowers of choice for the bridal bouquet and floral decorations. Everything was co-ordinated, from a private caterer to the wedding cake.

It had seemed an impossible challenge, but an eminently successful one, Lisane concluded as she admired the result with awe.

The weather was perfect, clear skies, warm early-summer sunshine, with barely the slightest breeze drifting in from the sea.

'Let's go do this, shall we?'

It took only minutes to descend the stairs and cross the marble-tiled floor to where the floor-to-ceiling glass doors stood open to reveal a manicured lawn, garden borders and miniature topiary.

A roll of cream carpet led to a rose-decorated arbour, where Zac stood waiting for her.

He was something else, his tall, broad-shouldered frame attired in an impeccably tailored dark suit.

Almost by instinct he turned towards her, and she felt as if her heart stood still for a few telling seconds before it kicked in to pulse at a rapid beat.

Clearly evident were the extent of Zac's emotions as she slowly trod the carpet towards him. It made her want to smile, laugh and cry...all at the same time.

'Wow.'

Solene encapsulated it in one softly spoken word.

Was it possible to walk on air? It certainly felt as if her feet didn't touch the ground.

The smile won out, lighting up her features and lending her eyes a luminous quality as she reached his side and interlinked her fingers with his own.

Without thought to anyone else, Zac lowered his head and laid his mouth gently against her own, savoured, then reluctantly withdrew to smile at the faint tinge of colour accenting her cheeks.

It was a beautiful ceremony. Those present endorsed and applauded it.

Although throughout Lisane's total focus was Zac, the look of love he made no attempt to hide, and the manner in which he promised to cherish and protect her all the days of his life as he placed a circlet of diamonds on the finger of her left hand.

Words she repeated to him in a clear, unwavering voice as she took his left hand and slid on a gold band.

Laughter, smiles and hugs were gifted and exchanged against the backdrop of sparkling ocean waters and blue sky.

There were photographs and celebratory champagne, which Lisane declined in favour of an innocuous mix, finger food, followed later by a sumptuous meal indoors.

Max and Felicity Winstone appeared genuinely delighted with their daughter-in-law, and the prospect of becoming grandparents.

Something for which Lisane was immensely grateful, and she said as much soon after they farewelled their four guests at the end of the evening.

Zac curved an arm around her waist as he led the way upstairs.

'Two sets of parents, the fathers respected associates and close friends, whose wives contrived a private dream.' He brushed a light kiss to her cheek. 'Allegra and I grew up in each other's shadow, friends but never lovers.'

Not for the want of trying on Allegra's part, Lisane thought quietly.

Except that was in the past, and she held the future in her hands.

There was only now, and all the tomorrows she'd share with the man who was the love of her life.

In slightly less than seven months there would be a child…a precious gift, uniquely theirs.

Life, she accorded with a satisfied sigh, was better than good.

It was a very special miracle.

'Tired?'

They reached the upper floor and turned towards their bedroom.

'It's been a wonderful day,' Lisane offered gently. 'Thank you.'

Zac lifted a hand and trailed light fingers down the edge of her jaw. 'We have the night.'

She turned her cheek into the palm of his hand. It was fun to tease a little, and she tilted her face towards his own. 'Mmm, is that an invitation or a promise?'

'Both.'

Her soft laughter captivated him, and in one fluid movement he lifted her into his arms and carried her to their suite.

'Caveman tactics, huh?'

He took the pins from her hair, and let the light weight fall onto her shoulders.

'Need,' Zac said softly. 'For you. Only you.'

Her eyes shimmered a little as she offered a tremulous smile. 'Me, too.'

Simple words from the depths of her heart.

BRIDES OF CONVENIENCE

**Forced into marriage—
by a millionaire!**

Read these four wedding stories
in this new collection by your
favorite authors, available in
Promotional Presents May 2007:

THE LAWYER'S CONTRACT MARRIAGE
by Amanda Browning

A CONVENIENT WIFE
by Sara Wood

THE ITALIAN'S VIRGIN BRIDE
by Trish Morey

THE MEDITERRANEAN HUSBAND
by Catherine Spencer

Available for the first time at retail outlets this May!

Silhouette®
Desire

Introducing talented new author
TESSA RADLEY
making her Silhouette Desire debut
this April with

BLACK WIDOW BRIDE
Book #1794
Available in April 2007.

Wealthy Damon Asteriades had no choice but to
force Rebecca Grainger back to his family's estate—
despite his vow to keep away from her seductive
charms. But being so close to the woman society once
dubbed the Black Widow Bride had him aching to
claim her as his own...at any cost.

On sale April from Silhouette Desire!

**Available wherever books are sold,
including most bookstores, supermarkets,
discount stores and drugstores.**

REQUEST YOUR FREE BOOKS!

HARLEQUIN® *Presents*®

2 FREE NOVELS PLUS 2 FREE GIFTS!

PASSION
GUARANTEED
SEDUCTION

YES! Please send me 2 FREE Harlequin Presents® novels and my 2 FREE gifts. After receiving them, if I don't wish to receive any more books, I can return the shipping statement marked "cancel." If I don't cancel, I will receive 6 brand-new novels every month and be billed just $3.80 per book in the U.S., or $4.47 per book in Canada, plus 25¢ shipping and handling per book and applicable taxes, if any*. That's a savings of close to 15% off the cover price! I understand that accepting the 2 free books and gifts places me under no obligation to buy anything. I can always return a shipment and cancel at any time. Even if I never buy another book from Harlequin, the two free books and gifts are mine to keep forever.

106 HDN EEXK   306 HDN EEXV

Name	(PLEASE PRINT)	
Address		Apt. #
City	State/Prov.	Zip/Postal Code

Signature (if under 18, a parent or guardian must sign)

Mail to the Harlequin Reader Service®:
IN U.S.A.: P.O. Box 1867, Buffalo, NY 14240-1867
IN CANADA: P.O. Box 609, Fort Erie, Ontario L2A 5X3

Not valid to current Harlequin Presents subscribers.

Want to try two free books from another line?
Call 1-800-873-8635 or visit www.morefreebooks.com.

* Terms and prices subject to change without notice. NY residents add applicable sales tax. Canadian residents will be charged applicable provincial taxes and GST. This offer is limited to one order per household. All orders subject to approval. Credit or debit balances in a customer's account(s) may be offset by any other outstanding balance owed by or to the customer. Please allow 4 to 6 weeks for delivery.

Your Privacy: Harlequin is committed to protecting your privacy. Our Privacy Policy is available online at www.eHarlequin.com or upon request from the Reader Service. From time to time we make our lists of customers available to reputable firms who may have a product or service of interest to you. If you would prefer we not share your name and address, please check here. ☐

HP07

Men who can't be tamed...or so they think!

Damien Wynter is as handsome and arrogant as sin.
He will lead jilted Sydney heiress Charlotte to the altar and
then make her pregnant—and to hell with the scandal!

If you love *Ruthless* men, look out for

THE BILLIONAIRE'S
SCANDALOUS MARRIAGE
by Emma Darcy

Book #2627

Coming in May 2007.

HARLEQUIN *Presents*

Dinner at 8

Wined, dined and swept away by a British billionaire!

Don't be late!

He's suave and sophisticated.
He's undeniably charming.
And above all, he treats her like a lady.

But don't be fooled....

Beneath the tux, there's a primal passionate lover
who's determined to make her his!

Gabriella is in love with wealthy Rufus Gresham,
but he believes she's a gold digger.
Then they are forced to marry.... Will Rufus use
this as an excuse to get Gabriella in his bed?

Another British billionaire is coming your way in May 2007.

WIFE BY CONTRACT, MISTRESS BY DEMAND
by Carole Mortimer

Book #2633

HPDAE0507